TOMB OF DOOM!!!

THE FOLLOWING MOVIE MYSTERY HAS BEEN APPROVED FOR

ALL AUDIENCES

BY THE GOOD PEOPLE AT WALKER BOOKS UK

THIS BOOK HAS BEEN RATED:

E	EPIC
SCENES OF AWESOME PYRAMIDS, REAL LIVE DEAD PEOPLE AND ONE THIEVING DOG	

Also by Tanya Landman

SAM SWANN'S MOVIE MYSTERIES
Zombie Dawn!!!

POPPY FIELDS IS ON THE CASE!
Mondays are Murder
Dead Funny
Dying to be Famous
The Head is Dead
The Scent of Blood
Certain Death
Poison Pen
Love Him to Death
Blood Hound
The Will to Live

MYTHS AND MAGIC
Waking Merlin
Merlin's Apprentice
The World's Bellybutton
The Kraken Snores

FOR YOUNGER READERS
Flotsam and Jetsam
Flotsam and Jetsam and the Stormy Surprise
Flotsam and Jetsam and the Grooof
Mary's Penny

FOR OLDER READERS
Apache
Buffalo Soldier
The Goldsmith's Daughter

SAM SWANN'S MOVIE MYSTERIES

TOMB OF DOOM!!!

TANYA LANDMAN

ILLUSTRATIONS BY
DANIEL HUNT

WALKER
BOOKS

First published 2014 by Walker Books Ltd
87 Vauxhall Walk, London SE11 5HJ

2 4 6 8 10 9 7 5 3 1

This book has been typeset in Stempel Schneidler

Printed and bound in Great Britain by Clays Ltd, St Ives plc

British Library Cataloguing in Publication Data: a catalogue record for this book is available from the British Library

ISBN 978-1-4063-3087-8

www.walker.co.uk

For Emma, for general all round brilliance

All the chapters in this book are named after movies.
This is how I rate them:

SAM SWANN'S BOARD OF FILM CLASSIFICATION	
BG — **BANNED BY GRAN** (Unseen by Sam)	F — **FANTABALISSIMO**
FF — **FANTASTICALLY FANTABALISSIMO**	FFF — **FANTASMAGORICALLY FANTASTICALLY FANTABALISSIMO**
WTA — **WET THURSDAY AFTERNOON** (Only watch if there's nothing better to do)	3A — **AVOID AT ALL COSTS**
W — **WEIRD**	RS — **RUBBISH SEQUEL** (Watch the original instead)
5Z — **ZZZZZ** (Sleep guaranteed)	EPS — **EYE-POPPINGLY SCARY**
WLI — **WATSON LOVES IT**	GGG — **GIGGLES GALORE GUARANTEED**

THE HISTORY BOYS  

Last month, zombies were the height of fashion: wall-to-wall rotting flesh with exposed hearts, spleens, livers, kidneys and miles of intestines spilling out all over the place. But things have changed. Dad's moved on to mummies. Now it's all about fragrantly embalmed bodies wrapped in clean linen bandages. Brains carefully hooked out through nostrils. Internal organs neatly removed and pickled in jars. Is this an improvement? Only time will tell…

Ralph Pitter as our fearlessly cool hero

Ben Silverman as the Hitler-worshipping baddie

Tinkerbelle Cherry as Dan Diamond's cute-as-cherry-pie daughter

You see, Dad is a Special Effects Make-up Supremo. He's in demand on movie sets all over the world and I get to go with him. According to child megastar Tinkerbelle Cherry, he's the best in the business. The reason for his latest obsession is that he's working on a new movie:

TOMB OF DOOM!!!

The action-packed plot goes something like this…

THE EPIC QUEST BEGINS...

Dan and Kitty Diamond are searching the desert for a lost tomb containing a legendary relic of awesome power. Bad guys are on their trail.

They find the entrance.

They have to fight their way past fire pits ...

... snakes ...

... and booby traps!

This belonged to Anubis himself. It has the power to open the door between this life and the next.

Could it bring Mummy back to life...?

I'm afraid not. The papyrus says ONE SOUL IN EXCHANGE FOR ANOTHER. I can't kill someone to save your mother.

Suddenly Dan is hit over the head.
THUD

Kitty is kidnapped and the relic is stolen.

Back at the bad guys' den...
I thought we was after the relic, not some kid. You said we could use it to fetch Hitler back from the dead.
You heard her father. We have to put one soul in to get one out.
Mmph! Mmph! Mmph!

You mean...?

Yep. The little lady is our payment plan. Kitty Diamond's going straight to hell.

As Kitty's an innocent child, her blood is pretty potent stuff. It only takes a single drop to open the door. Once that happens, it's not just Hitler who strolls through – every dead bad guy in history shows up. So it's deadly peril, gazillions of baddies and resurrected mummies all round. The logline says it's:

THE ULTIMATE BATTLE FOR THE ULTIMATE POWER!!!

If it sounds a bit *Indiana Jones*, that's because it is. The movie industry likes nothing better than repeating a successful format. Why else would they bother to do rubbish sequels of films like *Pirates of the Caribbean*?

MOVIE SEQUELS

So far there have been 10 Pink Panther films, 11 Star Treks, 23 James Bonds and 31 Carry On films. When *The Madness of King George III* was made into a movie it was renamed *The Madness of King George* because the film-makers didn't want the audience to think they'd somehow missed numbers *I* and *II*.

Logline
This sums up a film plot in one sentence.

Dad's in heaven, because unlike his last film, *ZOMBIE DAWN!!!*, this one definitely has The L Factor. Boxed Lego sets are rolling off production lines already, which means I'm friends with a mini-figure! How cool is that?

Tink and I met on location in Remotest Romania during the shoot for *ZOMBIE DAWN!!!* After a bit of trouble with an avenging ghost* we became friends. (Well, sort of. Tink's surprisingly brainy and very brave. But it's difficult to feel totally comfortable with someone whose idea of a good time is playing Barbie and Ken Take a Lot of Clothes With Them on Vacation.)

Most of *TOMB OF DOOM!!!* will be filmed on studio sets here in England, but a few crucial shots are being taken on location. In a couple of weeks, me and Dad are jetting off to the sand and sun of Egypt. There'll be pyramids and temples and mummies – real, live dead people! I've wanted to go to Egypt ever since

* You'll have to read *ZOMBIE DAWN!!!* to find out what happened.

Blue Peter did a feature about the discovery of Tutankhamen's treasure. I'm sure there are still loads of tombs out there in the desert just waiting to be dug up. Who knows what I might find? I can hardly wait.

Before that, Dad has to plan it all out so that when we get to Egypt everything's ready to go. Today he's meeting his make-up team and the wardrobe people in some posh office in London, and I have to go along with him. Not that Dad wants me at the meeting, but he's home schooling me and never misses an opportunity to Improve My Mind. The British Museum is just around the corner, so my task for the afternoon is to cram a few thousand years of ancient Egyptian history into my head.

Dad parks the car and points me in the right direction. We have to leave Watson* on the back seat because dogs aren't allowed in the museum. He's wearing Expression Number 10: *Deep Misery*. I have strict instructions to go straight to the brand-new-super-dooper-all-singing-all-dancing Egyptology exhibition and stay there until Dad rings me. For once, I don't care how long his meeting lasts. This is going to be fantabalissimo.

* Watson is my brother-from-another-mother: my best friend and the most loyal and obedient dog in the universe.

GODS AND MONSTERS  

This is what I'm expecting inside the museum:

This is what I get:

After about fifteen minutes I'm yawning my head off. My eyelids are sagging and I'm wondering how I'll get through the afternoon. I've developed a bad case of Museum Fatigue. Then I spot a room to the side of the main display. It has an extra large case in the centre, lit by a spotlight. I figure there must be something pretty special in there...

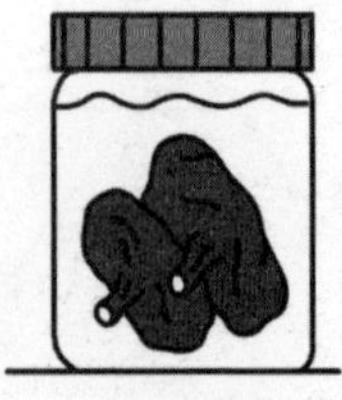

Jar of shrivelled kidneys?

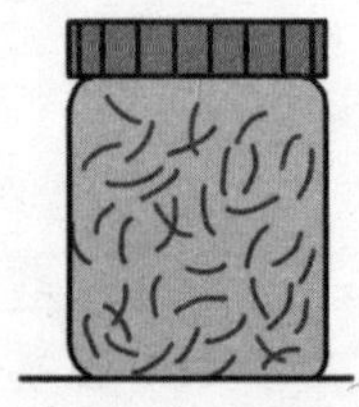

Pot of pharaohs' toenails?

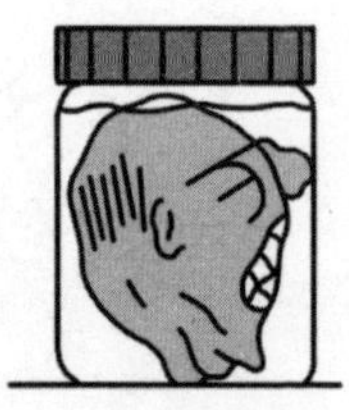

Disembodied head?

But it's just a bit of jewellery.

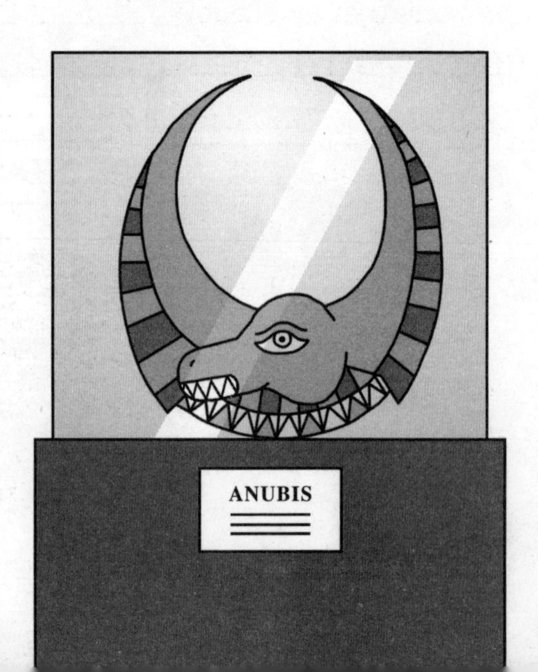

OK, so it's a pretty impressive bit of jewellery. It says on the label that Anubis oversees the soul's journey from this world to the next. I hadn't realized he was a dog. The necklace wouldn't be the cosiest thing to have hanging around your neck, but I'm not sure the ancient Egyptians were a very cosy bunch.

"Anubis." I say it out loud and the word echoes back at me. This is creepy, because:

1) it's freakily loud, and

2) the echo has a foreign accent.

Then I realize it's not actually an echo. There's someone else in the room. A man standing motionless in the shadows. He must have said "Anubis" a millisecond after I did. Only the way he said it made it sound like he was summoning up dark and mysterious forces. They should give him a part in *Tomb of Doom!!!*

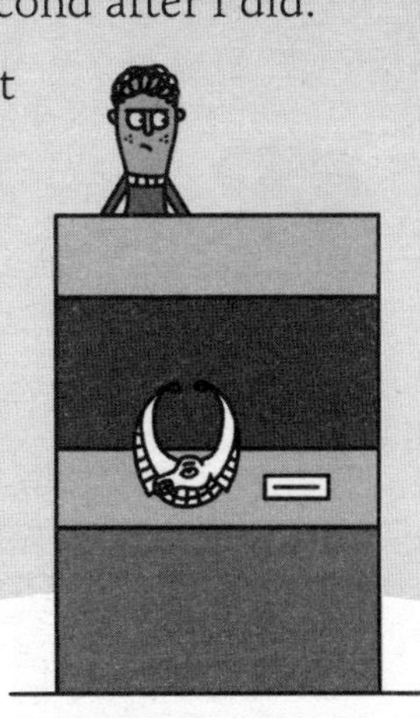

FREAKY PHOBIAS

Lots of movie stars have strange phobias. Billy Bob Thornton is scared witless by antique furniture. Orlando Bloom is afraid of pigs. Johnny Depp gets weirded out by clowns.

He grins and a couple of gold teeth catch the light. Cool, but strangely sinister. He comes across and stands by the case. Now he's between me and the way out.

"Anubis," he says again in that heavy accent. "You have heard of him?"

I nod and he looks genuinely delighted.

"You are interested in ancient Egypt?" he asks.

Now, you might be thinking that I shouldn't talk to strangers, but I've grown up on film sets, remember? You don't get any stranger than movie people.

Our conversation goes like this:

```
Sam:   Dad's told me to find out
       about Egyptian history.
```

We're flying there soon for his work.

Him: [Nostrils flaring a bit.] Your father is employed by an oil company perhaps?

Sam: No, he's in the movies. Target Films are shooting a film there called *Tomb of Doom!!!* We're going to Luxor first, then Cairo.

I start telling him about it but he's not paying attention. Which is strange. Normally if I mention that Dad's in the movie business, people's eyes go wide and immediately they want to know if I've ever met their screen idol…

But this guy's not interested in celebrities. He starts telling me about the necklace – only he calls it a collar.

* He's the dog in *The Artist*. Uggie possesses more talent than all of the actors in Hollywood put together.

He's just like Dad, seizing any opportunity to Educate and Inform a Young Mind.

"It was worn by the high priest when they buried Tutankhamen. *Tutankhamen*," he says again, licking his lips as if the name tastes delicious. "You know him?"

Well, not personally. But visions of *that* gold mask flit through my head. You'd have to have been living in an underground bunker on Mars for the last hundred years not to have seen a picture of it somewhere.

I nod.

By now, the strangely sinister man's hand is pressed flat against the glass case, as if the necklace is radiating heatwaves or magical power.

"Can you not picture the scene?" he says in a husky whisper. "The priest, his blood pulsing beneath this collar, his living flesh warming the stones as the murdered king is entombed…"

My voice comes out a bit higher and squeakier than usual. They never mentioned that on *Blue Peter*.

"Yes, murdered. Some say he was not, of course, but I am sure of it; I feel it here in my heart. Yet the crime remains unsolved."

I bet Sherlock Holmes could have solved it, I think. I might do some investigating while I'm in Egypt. Maybe me and Watson could take it on as a case. (I named Watson after Sherlock's sidekick. I'm training him to be a Sniffer Hound.)

But even if I worked out who'd done it, the murderer would be long dead. We'd have to dig him up to arrest him.

And my problems wouldn't be over yet. How could you put a mummy on trial?

The sinister guy interrupts my train of thought. Tutankhamen's murde may have happened 3,000 years ago but he is seriously obsessed with it. He's got one of those weird eyeglass things out now – the sort that jewellers use.

"The past is alive, is it not? It is with us, here in this room. The very air throbs with ancient energy. Can you not feel it?"

Erm ... no. And I'm trapped in the room with a weirdo. Brilliant.

Out of the corner of my eye, I look for possible escape routes.

Run like **Dash** in *The Incredibles*?

Swing from light flex to light flex like **Tarzan**?

Whistle for Watson to charge to my rescue like **Bolt**?

Then there's the squeak of heel on lino and I catch a glimpse of a museum guard in the next room. I relax a bit, until the Sinister Stranger suddenly draws a sharp intake of breath as if he's been stabbed. His eyes are popping with shock as he peers into the case and his face is screwed up in pain.

"No!" he croaks. "This isn't… It can't…!"

Finish your sentences, dude.

"Isn't *what*? Can't *what*?" I ask him.

He turns to me, and his face is white, like all the blood has drained out of him.

"It's not right…" he whispers. And then he yells it.

The guard comes running. Which is lucky for me; unlucky for him. Because the Sinister Stranger goes beserk, grabbing the front of his jumper and screeching into his face.

Being a museum guard must be a boring job. What is there to do all day except stop small children licking the glass cases? (They do, you know. I've seen them.) I reckon this one has been waiting all his life for this. Because he's got a big grin on his face when he throws the Sinister Stranger out of the museum.

BROTHER BEAR

THE ELGIN MARBLES

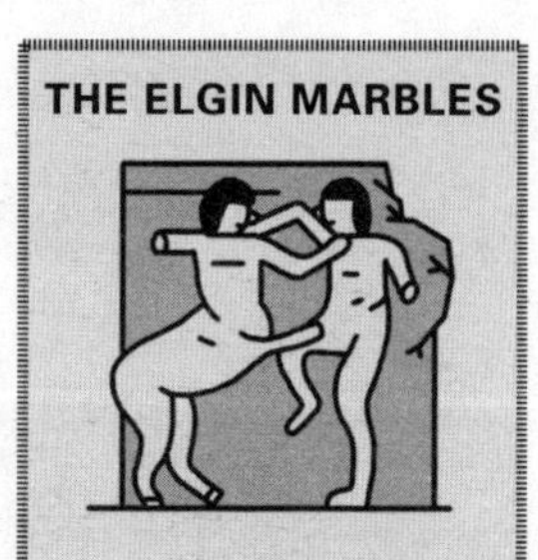

The Elgin Marbles were removed from the Parthenon in Athens and have been on display in the British Museum since 1817.

The afternoon is turning out to be pretty good. After the Sinister Stranger gets chucked out, the guard comes back and says to me, "What a nutter! Just like them Greeks wanting their marbles back."

"Marbles?" I say in surprise. I can't imagine anyone making a fuss about a few glass balls.

The guard laughs. "Not the kind of marble you're thinking of, I expect. They're in room 18. Carvings, taken from Greece by Lord Elgin a couple of hundred years ago. He said it was preservation; they said it was vandalism. The Greek and British governments are still arguing about it."

I look at the Anubis collar. "What's that got to do with this?"

> **MOVIE MEGABUCKS**
>
> *CLEOPATRA* was released in 1963 and for 15 years held the record for the most expensive film ever made. Taking inflation into account, it still comes out near the top of the list.

"He probably wants it returned to Egypt. I can't see why else he was getting so worked up, can you?" He shrugs, then goes back to his protecting-glass-cases-from-toddlers'-tongues duties, so I carry on wandering around the museum.

By the time Dad calls to say he's finished his meeting, I've learnt quite a lot.

British Museum Field Trip

Name: Sam Swann
Tutor: Mr Swann (aka "Dad")
Assignment: Learn about ancient Egypt

HISTORY

- Cleopatra was a real person, not just a character in a movie. (Who'd have believed it? Next they'll try and tell me the Titanic was a real ship!)
- Cleopatra got into a big fight with the Romans and lost. So she killed herself with an asp. (That's a snake – small but deadly.)
- When Tutankhamen's tomb was discovered in the Valley of the Kings, he cursed the people who had dug him up. Awesome.
- The Great Pyramid is the oldest and biggest one in Giza. For 4,000 years it was the tallest man-made structure on the entire planet. It's the only one of the Seven Wonders of the Ancient World that's still standing.

GEOGRAPHY

- The Valley of the Kings is near Luxor. Me and Dad are going there.
- Giza is near Cairo. We're going there, too.

In fact I've absorbed so much information, my head feels like it's going to burst. Luckily the brain-exploding disaster is averted when I get back to the car because Watson is so pleased to see me that I forget pretty much everything. I have violated Rule Number 1 of the Pack Brotherhood code. Watson starts with a little whining huffle and works all the way up to full-blown yelping.

Why did you leave me? I was abandoned!!!
I was so sad and so very, very, very, very lonely!
Oh why oh why oh why did you leave me?
Did I do something wrong? I am a very sorry dog
and whatever it was I won't do it again, not ever
never ever, because I love you I love you
I LOVE YOU I LOVE YOU!

THE RULES OF

PACK BROTHERHOOD

1
The pack must stick together at all times

2
The pack must share:
(a) toys
(b) bones
(c) beds

3
The pack must support each other in all circumstances

4
One pack member must never betray another

5
Pack brothers must watch each other's backs

6
Pack brothers must:
- play together
- roll around together
- eat and sleep together
- bark and howl together

I get into the back seat so he can sit on my lap. (He doesn't like cars much, so it is my duty as a pack member to keep him company.) Thirty kilos of labrador lands on me and all I can see is fur. And a tongue. A wet tongue. He's got it up my nose. *Aaaargh!* In my mouth. *Euw!!* I try to scrub my tongue clean with a tissue. Watson scoffs it. He is now in doggy heaven.

We haven't gone far when he starts growling and pawing at the window. Watson's a friendly animal, and it's so unusual for him to sound fierce that Dad and I both look around to see what the problem is.

We're now driving past the museum. There's a lot of shouting and a bunch of guards are pushing and shoving at the top of the steps. Then someone comes stumbling down them. It's the Sinister Stranger. The guards are yelling at him to get lost. It looks like he's been trying to go back in.

What is he like? I mean, really – ancient Egypt is interesting enough, but all that stuff happened ages ago. It's in the past.

He needs to get over it.

THE MUMMY BG EPS

The next day, Dad decides to mummify my corpse. Again. He's a perfectionist when it comes to special effects make-up and I'm his unpaid guinea pig. When he was working on *ZOMBIE DAWN!!!* I was killed in more ways than you can imagine. Shot, electrocuted, stabbed: you name it, I died it. I suffered more violent ends than Phil Connors in *GROUNDHOG DAY.*

I'd promised Watson a walk in the park first thing, but instead I'm stretched out on Gran's kitchen table almost completely wrapped in bandages.

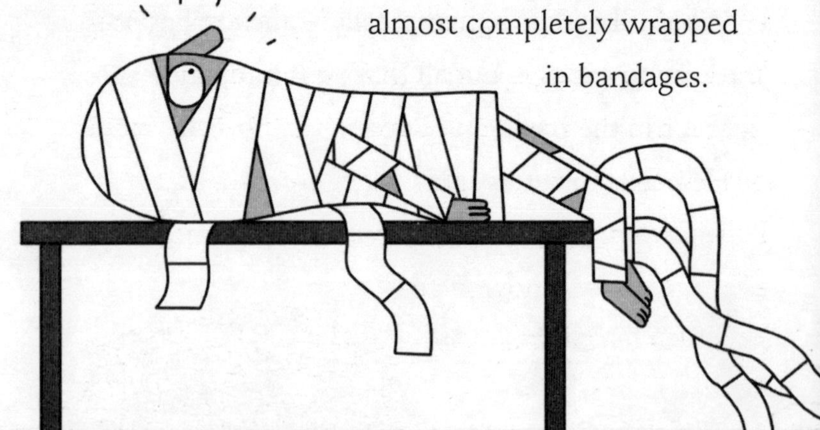

DEAD AGAIN

Phil Connors dies at least 11 times in *Groundhog Day*. Bill Murray – the actor who played the part – was bitten twice by the groundhog and had to have anti-rabies injections.

Dad has hooked my brain out through my nose and stuffed it into a canopic jar. Right now he's doing something weird to my face, trying to make me look like my skin's been turned into leather.

My dog is seriously depressed. Gran emptied the bin before she went out, so there are no smells to sniff. No leftovers to levitate. No packets to poach. Out of the corner of my eye I can see he's getting restless. And a restless Labrador is a dangerous thing. Uh-oh! He's spotted something. A piece of lacy material is poking through a gap in the laundry basket. Millimetre by millimetre he's edging across the floor towards it like a Canine Commando.

The freshly washed underwear had better watch out. Watson tortures tights. Slaughters socks. Pulverizes pants. He's got a murderous gleam in his eye. Any second now, he'll make his final assault.

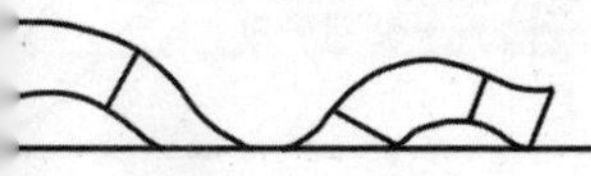

"Erm – Dad…"

Dad has Gran's hairdryer in his hand and is blasting me in the face with it.

"Shh. Hold still!"

"Dad!"

"I'm nearly done." Now he's holding a thermometer against my forehead. He doesn't notice Watson quietly take the lace in his teeth and begin to pull.

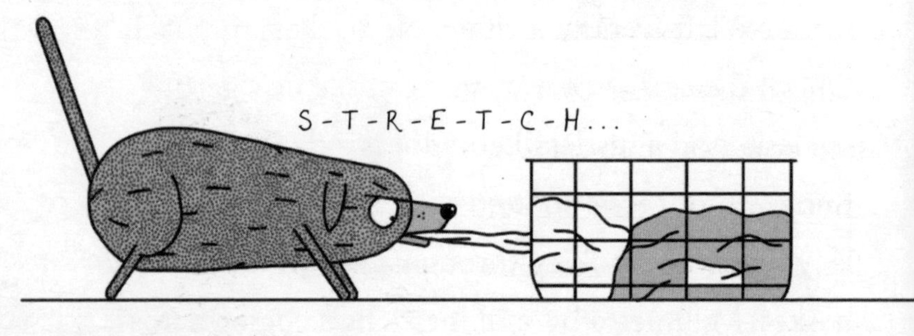

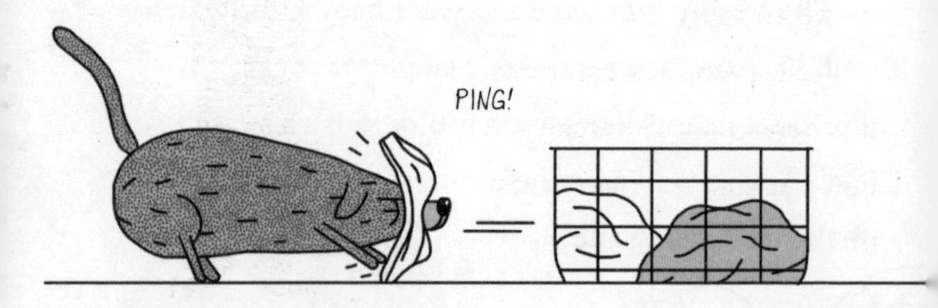

Two seconds later, my dog has Gran's pants in his mouth.

He throws them in the air and pounces on them when they land. He shakes them from side to side, growling savagely. And they're still not dead. So he throws them in the air again.

Well, even Dad can't miss it when a pair of knickers flies past his face. He yelps in alarm and tries to grab them.

The more Dad tries to catch him, the more Watson thinks it's a game. My arms and legs are bandaged so tightly, I can't move. I just have to lie there motionless while they run round and round the table. Then Gran gets back. When she sees what Watson's done to her pants, my dog nearly gets mummified for real.

DOG DAY AFTERNOON BG W

The Gran's Pants Incident has not been forgotten. Or forgiven. For the next two weeks, Watson and I are in Deep Disgrace. Gran's decided that Watson needs some serious training – and that I'm the boy for the job. She's bought me yet another book: *Perfect Pets Make Happy Homes*. Before we leave for Egypt, Watson has to learn to BEHAVE. If I don't succeed she's threatening to have him banged up in kennels until I get back, because she has officially HAD ENOUGH. (We're not allowed to take him with us because of the quarantine regulations.)

The problem is, my dog has the memory of a goldfish. According to the book, this whole training thing revolves around treats. It says, “Ignore the bad behaviour, reward the good.”

This is what is supposed to happen:

This is what actually happens:

The book is rubbish. So I try something else. Something which has never failed. The F word*.

* FOOD!

But the second I flash Watson a cheesy treat, everything else goes out of his head. He is learning nothing. My dog has a brain the size of a guppy's.

After a week things have improved. Sort of. He hasn't stopped stealing Gran's pants, but he doesn't run away with them any more. He's figured out:

Pants + Sam = Treat

Now he brings them straight to me so I can swap them for food. All I have done is train him to be a thief. Watson is now a Canine Criminal.

The day we leave for Egypt, Gran drops me and Dad off at the airport. I've made her promise not to put Watson in kennels, but she's looking shifty. And he looks miserable. If he can't stand a couple of hours in the car without his pack brother, how's he going to manage four weeks?

How am *I*?

AIRBORNE

The actors on *Tomb of Doom!!!* are American (apart from the bad guys – they're British, even though they live in Los Angeles).

The cast are all flying straight to Egypt from the States, but the film crew are mostly Brits and just about the whole plane is full of them. Everybody knows

each other from films they've worked on before, so there's a bit of a party atmosphere. There's a lot of backslapping and high-fiving Dad as he works his way down the aisle, and a lot of hair-ruffling and head-patting for me as I follow. It's enough to dislodge my brain. I wish I could bare my teeth and growl at them like my pack brother.

BAD BRITS

Hollywood loves British actors playing villains, especially if they put on a German accent, like Jeremy Irons and Alan Rickman in the *DIE HARD* films.

Cast and Crew
The cast are the actors in front of the camera. The crew are all the people behind it – the lighting and sound engineers, the production team, the make-up and wardrobe people, etc.

Dad's seat is right next to Anoushka, the wardrobe mistress; her assistant, Craig, is across the aisle. Dad's been working pretty closely with them both during pre-production and it takes all of three seconds for them to start talking about the shoot.

Pre-production
The period of movie-making before the actual shooting starts.

"Did you solve that problem with the foundation?" Anoushka asks Dad.

"Yep." Dad nods. "Tracked down a different brand. It should be fine."

"Think it will cope with the heat?" Anoushka wags a finger at Dad. "I don't want my costumes ruined if it melts. Lord alone knows what the laundry facilities will be like in Egypt."

"Well, it worked on Sam at any rate. Got it up to forty-five degrees and it held." (So that's why he was blasting my face with a hairdryer!) Dad is looking seriously sniffy about having his make-up techniques questioned. He asks Anoushka pointedly, "How about the collars? Did they arrive on time?"

Bor-ring!! It's more interesting listening to the safety drill. They do it in English and Arabic, and I manage to pick up some of the language. By the time we take off I know the words for "emergency exit", "crash-landing" and "Brace! Brace!" I am feeling pretty pleased with myself.

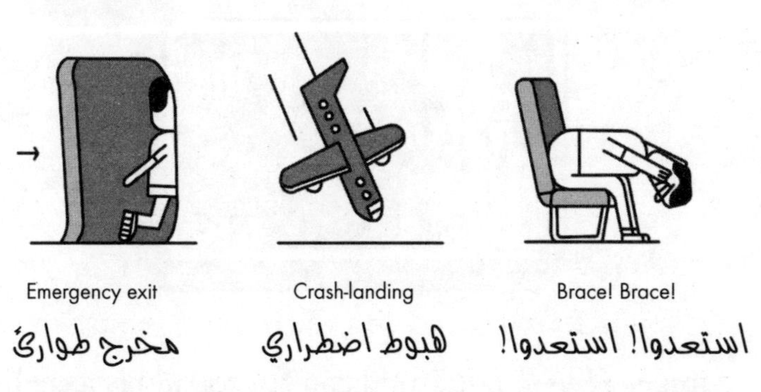

Dad and Anoushka are still banging on about work, so I pick up Dad's newspaper. On page five there's a bit about the British Museum being broken into – just the week before I was there.

THE DAILY

BUNGLED BREAK-IN BAFFLES BOFFINS

A smashed window and signs of forced entry alarmed curators at the British Museum when they arrived for work on Monday morning. However, fears for the museum's priceless treasures

Nothing was stolen, so it's not exactly sensational news. I'm about to die of boredom when the food arrives. Then I have something proper to think about. Like what exactly is *that* supposed to be?

Impossible to tell. And I can't ask Dad because he's still talking to Anoushka and shovelling food into his mouth – regardless of whether it's animal, vegetable or mineral.

Well, whatever it is, it doesn't taste too bad. Doesn't taste of anything, actually.

Eventually we land, and then there's all the hassle of getting our suitcases back. Usually we'd have to get Watson from the oversized baggage area, but this

time we don't. I get dog-
sick*, especially when I hear one howling somewhere outside the terminal building.

Dad must know what I'm thinking, because he says, "He'll be fine, Sam. Come on, let's get going."

As soon as we're out of the air-conditioned terminal, the heat hits us. It's almost as bad as the *Headhunters of Borneo* shoot. That was in the jungle and the air was like a warm wet flannel. This is different – a dry desert heat, more like being blasted with a zillion hairdryers (and I know all about that).

---

* This is like being homesick, only worse.

As there were so many of the crew on the flight, Target Films has hired a coach to transport us to the hotel. It takes maybe half an hour and all the way there's sand, sand, SAND as far as the eye can see. It's like the biggest beach ever (although it has to be said, the sea is a *very* long way out). Things have suddenly got exciting. The sun is blazing down from a blindingly bright blue sky.

Then we arrive at the hotel and there's a big black cloud hanging over it. (Not literally. Figuratively*.) The atmosphere is tense to say the least. When we step into the lobby we find out why.

Tinkerbelle Cherry has flown in from Los Angeles. And she's in a Seriously Bad Mood.

---

* Good word. Means the opposite of "literally".

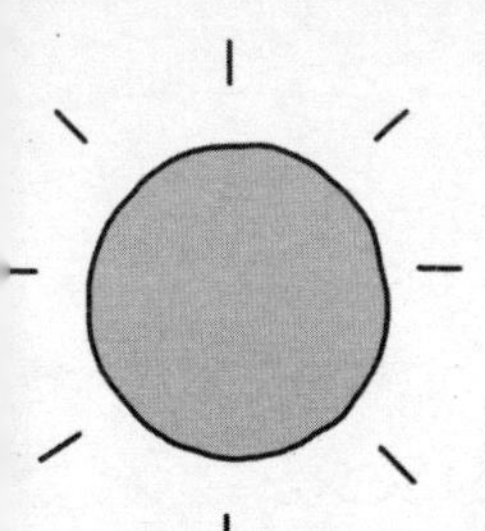

STAR WARS

Tinkerbelle Cherry is the child star of heartwarming family favourites like *Gnome at Home*, *Gnome Alone* and *Gnome Is Where the Heart Is*. Then she broke out of Cute mould by taking the lead in *Zombie Dawn!!!*, in which her character sucked people's brains out through a straw.

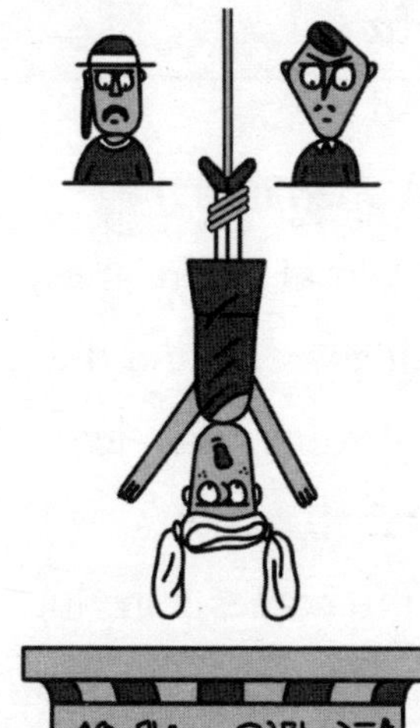

In *Tomb of Doom!!!* Tink gets to be dangled upside down over a sacrificial altar by Heston Schweinhund and the Bad Guys, who want to cut her still-beating heart from her chest. Some people have all the luck.

Meanwhile, me and Dad have stepped into the lobby of an extremely classy hotel. Wow! There are massive pillars, and pot plants as tall as trees, and the floor is solid marble – as smooth and shiny as an ice rink. Perfect for skating across. Fantabalissimo!

Before I can give it a go, Tink's mum comes hurrying across the lobby. I think she's heading for Dad, but she

totally ignores him and grabs me by the arm instead.

"Sam! Am I glad to see you! Tink's been asking over and over when you're getting here. Can you come straight up?"

Mrs Cherry looks mega-stressed.

I say, "Yeah, OK. Is that all right, Dad?"

"Sure. I'll fetch you once I've checked us in."

Tink hurls herself at me before her mum has even closed the door. It's dead embarrassing.

"Erm ... hi, Tink," I say, trying to prise her arms off my waist. "You OK?"

"No, I'm not! I'm vewy, vewy cwoss!"

It takes me a couple of seconds to translate. "You're *cross*? Why?"

She lets me go (big relief!), stamps her foot and pouts. "They won't let me have any kittens."

Ah. OK. I get it.

When you're a Hollywood megastar, you can demand anything you like from the film company.

DIVA DEMANDS

Barbra Streisand demands a scattering of rose petals in her toilet bowl and Cher needs a wig room.

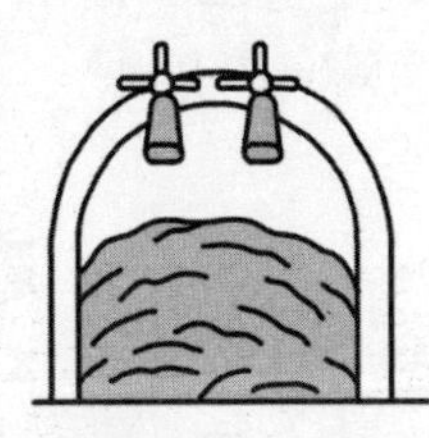

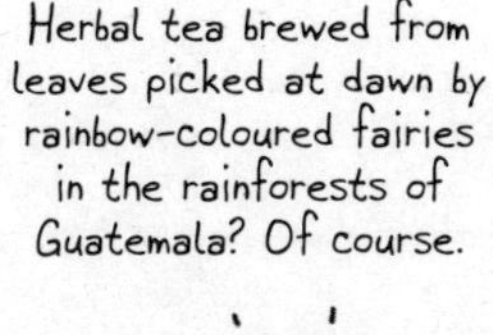

Although Tink's demands mostly involve access to a whole swarm of Barbies, her contract also says she has to have five real, live kittens to play with when she's not working. But even Hollywood megastars can't get around some things.

"Thilly, thilly rules! They said it's because of wabies."

"Rabies? Tell me about it! I had to leave Watson at home too."

"No! Poor Tham!" Her eyes fill up with tears. She looks like she's about to hug me again so I take a step back, but she doesn't, she just looks sympathetic. She's no substitute for my pack brother, but maybe her company is better than nothing.

Or maybe not.

"Never mind," she says. "I've got lots of new Barbies." Like a magician pulling a rabbit from a hat she produces a sparkly box. "Look! The Twilight thet. I'll be Bella. You can be Edward!"

VALLEY OF THE DOLLS  

Luckily for me, Tink's in such a stinking mood over the kittens that she's happy to ditch her "Let's do a complete rerun of the whole Twilight series" idea and go along with my "Bella and Edward are rulers of ancient Egypt" instead. When I tell her that in real life Tutankhamen was murdered, she gets quite excited and decides that Bella and Edward have to die too. Both of them get beheaded in a violent revolt led by an army of pink teddies. It's brutal.

THE TEDDY UPRISING

A LONG TIME AGO, IN A
KINGDOM FAR, FAR AWAY,
THE TEDDIES WERE REVOLTING.

Once Bella and Edward have been beheaded, they need to be embalmed. Brains have to be pickled, organs removed. It's all very Educational. Tink grabs a roll of toilet paper, and we're wrapping it around them, mummy-style, when Dad shows up.

Everyone is eating in the hotel restaurant before turning in for the night. The crew have got a really early start tomorrow. But Tink doesn't eat with mere mortals. She has her own personal chef who prepares nutritionally-balanced-for-a-growing-girl macrobiotic slop just for her. She asks me to stay for dinner but I ignore the pleading look in her eyes. I've sampled it once and I'm never eating brown rice and tofu again if I can help it. Even Watson turned his nose up at it, and he's the kind of dog that eats tissues. *Used* tissues.

I get up to leave.

Tink's eyes go all shiny. When she looks at me her lower lip starts to tremble. "Will you come on thet tomorrow, Tham?"

"Yeah, OK," I say, diving through the door before she can hug me again. "See you then."

THE TEMPLE OF DOOM (RS)

Down in the restaurant, everyone's buzzing with anticipation. But as soon as they finish, the cast and crew all disappear off to get some sleep before the first day of the shoot. Me and Dad are tucked up in our beds by 7.42 p.m.

I can't wait for the morning. Scenes are never filmed in the order they appear in the final movie. The shoot for *Zombie Dawn!!!* began at the end with the last battle and then worked backwards. *Tomb of Doom!!!* is the same. When it's finished, the climax will look like this:

#308 The mummies awaken

ToD

Long shot of the temples of Karnak at sunrise, some tiny figures making their way through the pillars.

Camera zooms in and pans along the procession of bad guys dressed as ancient Egyptians.

A close-up of Kitty Diamond (Tink), bound and gagged.

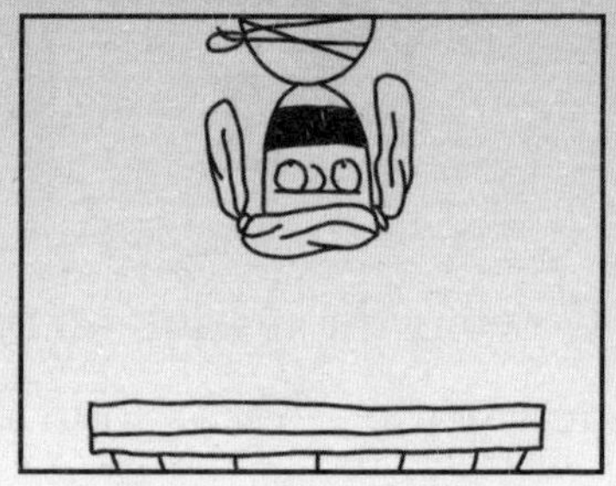

Camera pans out to wide shot. Kitty is suspended over the sacrificial altar.

Close-up of the knife that is about to cut her chest open.

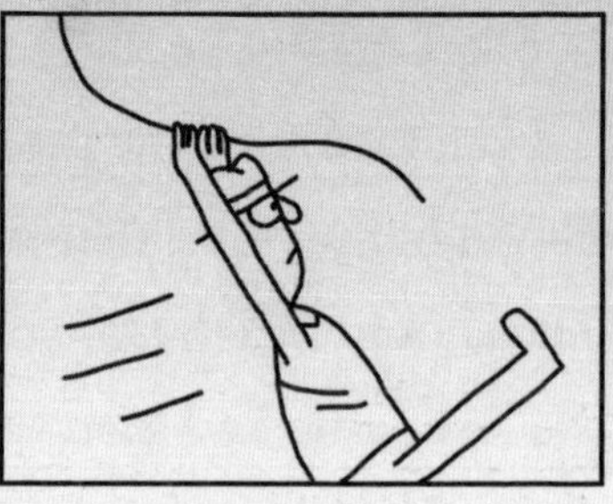

Cut to shot of Dan Diamond swinging from a pillar like Tarzan.

#308 The mummies awaken

ToD

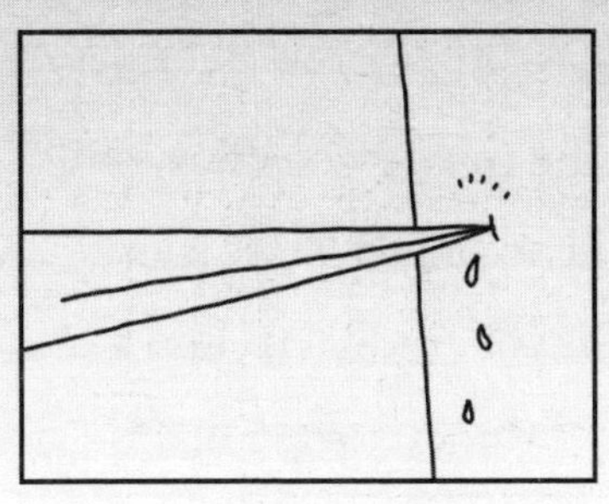

Extreme close-up of knife nicking Kitty's skin and a drop of blood spilling out.

Wide shot of temple columns going down like dominoes.

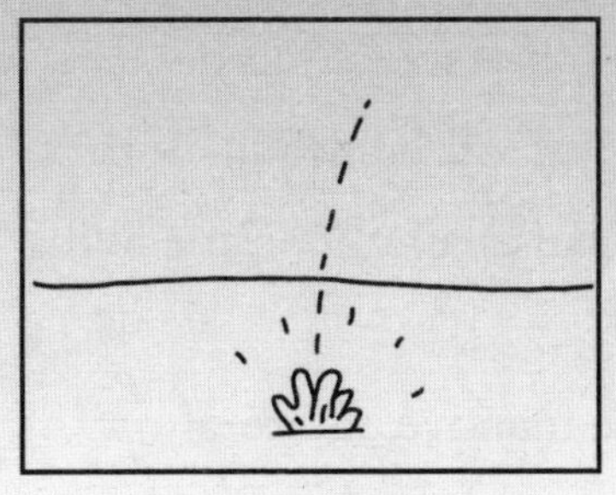

Extreme close-up of drop of blood splashing onto altar.

Wide shot – portal to underworld opens and a 100-foot Anubis steps through.

Mummies in undiscovered tombs rise out of the desert.

In museum, mummies awaken and throttle guards.

SOB STORY

To squeeze realistic emotional reactions out of his child actors in *ET*, director Steven Spielberg shot the scenes in the right order (almost unheard-of). It worked – in the final scene Elliott is crying his eyes out for real.

It's all very *AVENGERS ASSEMBLE*. But sadly the movie goes downhill after that. The only way to close the portal is for Anubis to find a willing sacrifice. So sweet little Kitty Diamond does the decent thing and goes with him to the underworld. But Anubis is so touched by her selflessness that he allows her to leave the kingdom of the dead – with her mother! Both return to Dan Diamond in the living world. It's soppier than *ET*.

The sequence involves the massive and total destruction of:

The Karnak temples The Valley of the Kings The Avenue of Sphinxes

Obviously the Egyptian tourist board aren't keen on having their famous monuments blown up, so those bits will be filmed on studio sets back in the

UK. Plus there are all sorts of scale models under construction, and guys are hard at work sweating over hot computers and creating the CGI sequences. It will all get stuck together when the movie is edited. But tomorrow, the director, Blake Ford, wants to get the opening shot. He's going to film the real, actual sun coming up over the real, actual desert and lighting up the real, actual temple – with Dan Diamond watching the bad guys lead Kitty towards the altar.

The real, actual sun

CGI
Computer-generated imagery. (Dad calls the CGI guys Geeks with Gizmos.)

The window of opportunity for this take is limited, as not even a film director as powerful as Blake Ford can tell the sun, "Stop! Hold it right there. Can you go back down and then come up again, only this time with *feeling*?"

The real, actual desert

DAWN OF THE DEAD

BG EPS

Dad shakes me awake at 2.30 a.m. – that's TWO-THIRTY IN THE MORNING! – and tries to force-feed me cereal bars.

"Let me sleep," I groan. "I want to stay here."

"You promised Tink," Dad reminds me.

"She won't mind." I roll over and stuff my head under the pillow.

"Oh no you don't," says Dad. "A promise is a promise. If you put her in a bad mood, we're all done for. You're coming on set with me right now, sunshine."

It's no good protesting. Dad is like a sports coach.

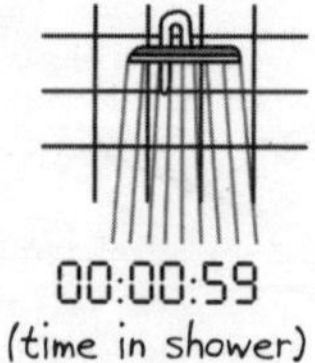

00:00:13
(time brushing teeth)

Then we're off, sprinting down the hotel corridors to meet the rest of the crew in the lobby before being bused to base*. (Tink, Ralph Pitter and Ben Silverman get an extra hour in bed and will be taken there in chauffeur-driven limos. That's megastar status for you.)

When we arrive at base I'm still half asleep, but even I can tell that things are more chaotic than they should be. It turns out that Anoushka's been taken ill in the night with some horrible stomach bug.

* This is where the film company parks all the trailers during a location shoot. Like a high-tech caravan site.

POISONED CHALICE

When they were shooting *RAIDERS OF THE LOST ARK*, the cast and crew got food poisoning. In the scene with the swordsman, Indiana is supposed to flick the weapon out of his enemy's hands with his whip, but Harrison Ford was too ill to do the stunt. That's why he shoots the guy instead. The only person who didn't get sick was director Steven Spielberg, who ate nothing but the tinned spaghetti he'd brought with him.

This means they're one down in the wardrobe trailer – which is a problem, as this first scene involves some complicated costumes. Craig is looking pasty-white and stressed. I offer to lend a hand – I mean, how difficult can it be to do up a few buttons? But my kindness and generosity don't appear to be appreciated. I just get a look of horror and a hasty, "No! I mean – no thanks, Sam. Nice of you, but no. No!"

Honestly! One no would have been enough. Then Craig mutters under his breath:

Never in a million years!
Not after *SHANGHAI SPACEMAN*.

That is *so* unfair! I only wanted to see what the costume looked like on. It wasn't my fault the zip got stuck.

SPACEMAN SAM

I thought that tube was oil. How was I supposed to know it was superglue?!

The crew are up against the clock now – or up against the sunrise, anyway. All I can do is keep out of the way. I tuck myself into a corner of Dad's make-up trailer and try to get some more sleep. I'm dozing, having a long and complicated dream in which a gigantic Anubis is chasing me through a massive sandpit while Tutankhamen and the cast of *TWILIGHT* cheer him on, when a small, gold-sandalled, perfectly manicured foot gives me a nudge.

"Hi, Tink."

"Thanks for coming, Tham." She sounds genuinely grateful that I got up in time. So she should. It's still only 4.50 a.m.

> **COSMIC!**
> Some Egyptian jewellery is out of this world – literally. When scientists blasted neutrons and gamma rays at a 5,000-year-old necklace, they discovered the iron beads had originally come from meteorites!

I rub my eyes and try to wake up properly. Tink looks amazing. Dad's made her face up with painted eyes like Cleopatra. She's wearing a black wig and a shimmering dress with golden amulets up her arms.

But here's the weird bit: around her neck is the Anubis collar I saw in the British Museum.

THE JEWEL OF THE NILE

"I saw it in the British Museum a couple of weeks ago!" I exclaim. "There was this weird guy who was completely obsessed with the thing."

"Don't be thilly, Tham," Tink says, running her fingers over the bared teeth of Anubis. "This isn't the real one. It's a weplica."

"I know that," I say quickly. "But why are *you* wearing it?"

"You've read the scwipt, haven't you? It's the welic they've all been looking for: the key to the portal."

Tink's smirking like a cat. "Isn't it tewwific? It really helps me get the feel of my part."

It's just as well Tink's in the zone, because the sky is starting to lighten and everyone has to get in position.

There's no scary music (that will get added in the editing suite) but it still sends shivers down my spine when the first rays of sunlight hit the temple. In the museum all that ancient history seemed dead and gone, but here it's alive and well. The sun has lit those pillars every morning for thousands of years. Pretty impressive.

> **Editing Suite**
> This is a room full of high-tech equipment where the film gets made into the finished version.

Tink does her bit brilliantly. Movie acting's a weird thing. She doesn't have to say anything in this scene – she barely has to move – yet even from where I'm standing she looks small and defenceless and you can tell Kitty Diamond's scared stiff. When Tink does stuff like that you can see why she earns so much.

They do four takes in quick succession and then the sun gets too high for them to carry on. It all looked great to me, but Blake isn't satisfied. He wants to go through the whole performance again tomorrow.

COSTUME COPIES

The wardrobe department always keeps spares of everything. For *RAIDERS OF THE LOST ARK* Indiana Jones had 10 identical leather jackets.

Meanwhile, it's still only 7.30 a.m. and the rest of the day lies ahead. They're shooting a scene with Ralph Pitter, Ben Silverman and the rest of the bad guys next, but Tink isn't needed for that so she's officially off duty. Target

Films has organized a catering trailer, and while I leg it over there to see what's on offer, Tink goes off to get changed back into normal clothes (well … as normal as a Hollywood diva can get). I'm on my third bacon and egg butty when she comes back and I see she's still wearing the Anubis collar.

"Tinky, honey," frets her mother, trailing along behind her. "Are you sure you should be wearing that?"

"Pretty" isn't the word I'd have chosen, but it is awesome; I can see why Tink likes it.

"OK, sweetie." Her mum gives Tink a hug. Then she looks at me like this:

Uh-oh. Something's up.

"Tinky," says Mrs Cherry, "I've had a word with Sammy's daddy..."

Sammy? SAMMY???!!!

Worse is to come.

"He says we can keep Sammy with us all day. Isn't that wonderful?"

When did this happen? Thanks a bunch, Dad.

Tink's mum looks from me to Tink and back again. "What do you two cherubs want to do now?"

Tink's in favour of going back to the hotel and playing with the Barbies, but I've got a better idea. I happen to know we're quite near the Valley of the Kings, where Tutankhamen was buried.

It doesn't take much to convince Mrs Cherry that a trip to the pharaohs' tombs will be Highly Educational. A child actor is only allowed to be on set for so many hours each day. Like me, Tink has school work to do. As far as Tinky's mummy is concerned, going to the Valley of the Kings will keep us occupied and fill our heads with Learning and Wisdom.

As for me – maybe this is my big chance to dig up a mummy of my very own.

VALLEY OF THE KINGS

Dad is delighted with the plan. He says he'll see me back at the hotel later and leaves me in Mrs Cherry's care. In a matter of minutes we're all sitting in the chauffeur-driven limo that Target Films has hired for Tink. We're going to visit King Tut in style.

Tink isn't allowed fizzy drinks on account of her brown-rice-and-cardboard diet, so the in-car drinks cabinet is stuffed with strange-coloured, weird-smelling fruit and vegetable smoothies. *Euw*. But the air-conditioning makes up for it. When we step out of the car at the other end, the heat hits us in the face like a brick.

Tink's mum has come fully prepared, but everything she's brought is with Tink in mind. Pink. Floral. Sparkly. By the time I'm ready to go, I look completely ridiculous.

But hey, this is still going to be amazing! Tink's mum stays in the car: she's claustrophobic, apparently, and can't bear to go underground. Neither can Donna, Tink's PA, or Trudi, Tink's stylist. So me and Tink head off to explore alone.

Not completely alone, obviously. Tink is a megastar: she can't go anywhere without protection. Right now this involves two beefy bodyguards called Chuck and Butch.

The Valley of the Kings is massive but we find Tutankhamen's tomb without too much trouble. There's a long tunnel and four separate chambers with peeling paintings on the walls. All the gold artefacts and precious relics and mummies and *that* mask are in the city museum in Cairo, but we're going there once filming's finished at the temple, so I'll still get to see them.

Meanwhile, it's good being in the actual place where King Tut was buried. But it's hot down here and it's getting more and more crowded. Pretty soon the whole place is stuffed with sweating tourists and Tink's had enough, so we decide to head back out. I'm just about to tell her the story of Tutankhamen's curse when suddenly the tomb gets darker. My arms prickle with goose bumps. Then I see it's because a couple of Americans are coming down the passageway and they're both so big, they're blocking out the light.

They're having some sort of argument.

Woman: We're flying to England tomorrow, Teddie. If we don't get it tonight, we won't get it at all.

Man: Just relax, would ya? Everything's under control.

Woman: Oh yeah? You call a dose of food poisoning "under control"?

Man: [Weary.] It's not the end of the world, Jeanie. If we can't do it here, there are other places. The deal's done.

Woman: It might be signed and sealed, honey, but it sure ain't been delivered.

Man: [Angry.] I told you already! I'll get it sorted!

Me and Tink flatten ourselves against the wall and try to squeeze past. But just then a shaft of light hits Tink's Anubis collar.

Woman: [Gasp!] What on...?

Man: [Shoves his face in Tink's.] Hey, kid. Where in the heck did you get THAT?

STAR KID F

For one second, maybe two, there's a hushed silence. Tink looks startled but then recovers and explains haughtily that it's a "weplica".

The man chuckles. "**Hey, I'm sorry, kid. It gave me quite a turn, seeing that thing staring right at me!**"

"**It's awesome,**" croons the woman, reaching out to test the sharpness of Anubis's teeth. "**Wherever did you buy it, sugar?**"

Tink's in a bit of a huff. Sniffily, she mentions the film, and the Americans do this:

I suppose that in the dim light they didn't recognize her. When they take a closer look at Tink's face and realize they're in the presence of a megastar, both of them start hyperventilating.

"Tinkerbelle Cherry! Who'd have believed it?"

"I just loved *GNOME ALONE*, didn't I, Teddie?"

"You did! Jeanie cried so much at the ending, she nearly flooded the movie theatre! But hey, so did I!"

"I hate to trouble you, Miss Cherry, but might I have your autograph...?"

Now Tink has been spotted, it's not just the American couple who want her autograph, it's everyone in the burial chamber. And by the time we finally escape into the daylight, word has spread.

It seems the living Tinkerbelle Cherry is a way bigger attraction than the dead Tutankhamen. Butch and Chuck hold Tink's fans in line and Tink's mum, Donna and Trudi rush over to help, but it still takes more than two hours to prise Tink free from her admirers.

By the time we climb into the limo, the sun is high in the sky and the heat is punishing. Me and Tink reckon we've done enough ancient history for one day and head to the hotel. I'm steeling myself for an afternoon of *TWILIGHT* re-enactments, but luckily for me, Tink's wrist has gone limp from all the signing and she hasn't got the strength to hold a Barbie.

All either of us is fit for now is a session in the hotel swimming-pool.

To begin with, Tink and I aren't exactly poolside soul mates.

Her idea of appropriate behaviour is this:

Mine is this:

But Tink soon comes round to my way of thinking.

MIRAGE (W)

It's a conspiracy. Dad and Tink's mum have been plotting. They've got it all worked out between them.

For as long as we're in Luxor, the routine will be the same. I'll get up up at 2.30 a.m. to watch the filming. Then, when Tink's done her bit on set, the two of us will be Educated through a series of visits to ancient sites. Dad expects me to take notes on where we've been and what we've seen so I can tell him about it when he's finished working.

Over the next five days we visit …

… and every tomb and temple in between.

This would be great fun if we hadn't arrived in the middle of a heatwave. The desert is boiling my brain. It's like in those old films when people are lost and they're crawling through the sand, going, "Water, water!" and then they see an oasis and run towards it, only it turns out to be a mirage.

When I'm not fantasizing about palm-fringed oases I'm imagining ancient Egyptian jackal-headed death gods. Everywhere we go, I swear I catch a glimpse of Anubis out of the corner of my eye. Then I turn my head for a better look and he's not there. Freaky, huh?

Luckily, at around lunchtime each day Mrs Cherry whisks us back to the hotel pool to cool down. The other guests are really thoughtful. When they see me and Tink coming, they leave so we can have the place all to ourselves.

On Day 6 Blake finally declares that he's satisfied with what he's shot. We're moving on up to Cairo in the morning. Dad starts cramming make-up into boxes in his trailer while Mrs Cherry takes me and Tink straight to the hotel to pack. I can't imagine how long it will take Tink's staff to pack her stuff. It takes me all of ten seconds to pack mine.

Once that's done, I've got the rest of the day to myself. I still haven't had a chance to try

out the marble floor in the hotel lobby, so I head downstairs and spend the next hour skating across it in my socks. I can get up a really good pace if I run down the stairs before I go into slide mode. I reckon I'm getting close to a land speed record when one of the waiters trips and I'm sent back to my room by the hotel manager. Stupid man. It's not my fault the waiter wasn't watching where he was going.

THE SHIPPING NEWS (BG) (5Z)

At 5 a.m. the next morning we head towards Cairo. Target Films has booked a luxury cruise liner to take us up the Nile so that Blake can get some "atmospheric" shots of Dan Diamond playing on deck with his sweet little daughter with all that desert in the background. Ralph and Tink will be kept busy, and Dad will be dusting them both with powder* in-between takes, so I'll have to amuse

* This isn't exactly a challenging job for Dad – one of his assistants could do it. But Tink "inthists". She wants the best in the business. She is what Gran would call "a right madam".

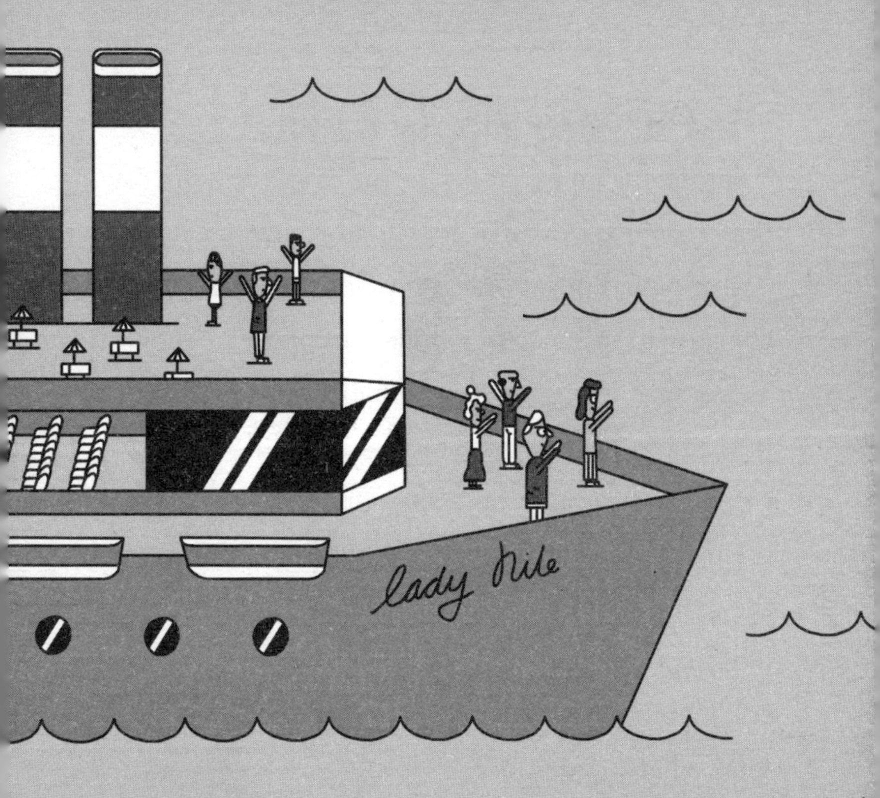

myself. It won't be hard to find things to do. This boat is so seriously well equipped, I want to live here permanently.

Me and Dad have an excellent cabin and there's room service on board that delivers my breakfast on a silver tray. I can lie in bed and watch palm trees and bulrushes slide past the window as I munch toast. Does life get any better than this?

Dad has written out a whole page of comprehension exercises for me to get on with, but they have a bit of an unfortunate accident. I figure I've had enough Education for the time being. As far as I'm concerned, this is major chilling out time.

Not that everyone gets a chance to appreciate the joys of life afloat. Anoushka's still so ill she had to be carried to her cabin on a stretcher, where she stays for the duration of the voyage. When she was heaved up the gangplank I saw that her skin was grey and loose-looking – like she'd lost loads of weight. But she was still jabbing her finger at Craig and telling the poor man what to do.

Dad isn't having an easy time either. Whenever Blake goes for a shot, an annoying motor boat comes into view.

At the end of Day 1, Dad is practically tearing his hair out. And it isn't any better on Day 2. On Day 3 I'm heading to the games arcade when I catch sight of the boat myself. There's only one guy on board and he's got slicked-back hair and a black suit. He looks like the man I saw in the British Museum, but it can't be. It's just the Egyptian heat doing my head in.

I mean, he couldn't possibly have followed me and Dad all the way to Egypt.

TO CATCH A THIEF (F)

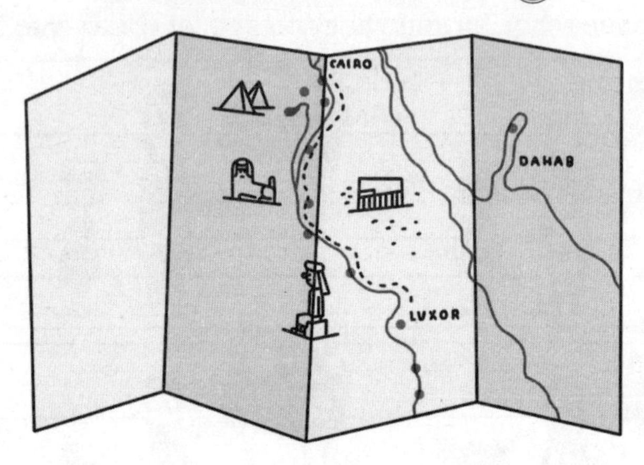

It takes four and a half days to cruise from Luxor to Cairo. At mid-morning on Day 4 the motor boat has disappeared and Blake finally gets his shot of Tink and Ralph. After that, Tink's allowed to have some W&W* time, and once she's got out of her Kitty Diamond costume and grabbed her swimming gear, we head off. Butch and Chuck are off duty because there's no one on board other than the cast and crew of *TOMB OF DOOM!!!*

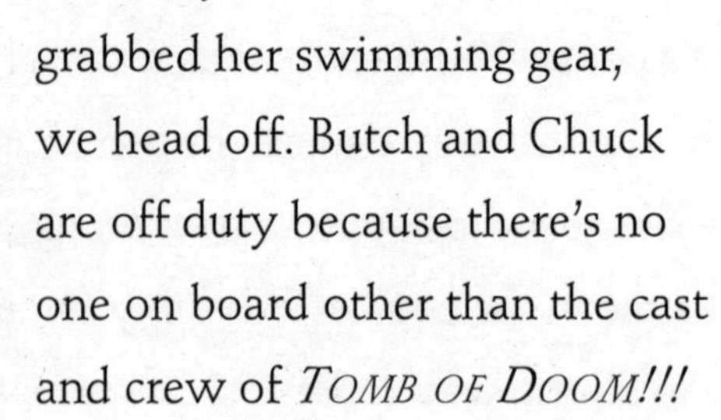

* West and Welaxation.

so she won't get harassed by fans or stalkers. It's nice to have a break from the sound of knuckles cracking manfully.

We're on our way to the pool and passing Anoushka's cabin. The door's ajar and we can see in the mirror that she's sitting up in bed. She looks a bit better, which would be good if she wasn't having a blazing row with Craig.

Hearing her name, Tink drops to the ground like she's in *Spy Kids* and tugs at the bottom of my T-shirt until I do the same.

BALD BOND

Sean Connery started losing his hair when he was 21, so he's wearing a toupée in all the Bond films he starred in.

She is *such* a drama queen! But hey, it's fun wriggling along on our elbows to get closer to the door, then plastering ourselves flat against the wall so we can't be seen. Sherlock Holmes would be proud of us. So would James Bond. We are behaving like true professionals. Not that we hear anything interesting.

Anoushka:	Suppose she wrecks it? If I have to get a replacement made, it's coming out of your wages.
Craig:	But there's a spare!
Anoushka:	No, there isn't!
Craig:	I thought I saw...

Anoushka: I'm on a budget here, Craig! Those replicas cost an arm and a leg. One of each is all I had done. If Tinkerbelle damages that collar, it will take weeks to get another. The whole shooting schedule would be thrown out.

Tink goes pale at the thought of the schedule being upset. She's been in the movies long enough to know that this would be a Very Bad Thing. I can see she's thinking of going straight back to her cabin so she can take the collar off right away. Then this happens:

Craig: She's being very careful...
Anoushka: She's a kid! Kids break stuff.

Ouch! Tink doesn't like that one bit. Actresses are SOOOO touchy! She rises to her full height –

all 3 foot 11 of it – and I can see she's about to march right in and Have It Out with Anoushka, when Craig whimpers squeakily, "Do you want me to have a word with her?"

The wardrobe mistress sighs heavily. "No. There's no point upsetting the little cow." Little cow?! Double ouch!! Tink is now officially Furious. But she doesn't want to get caught eavesdropping. She stalks off down the corridor towards the pool, noiseless as a cat, and I tiptoe along after her.

I have a bit of a swim while Tink sits on the side *glowering*.

And the day is about to go even further downhill. When we get back to Tink's cabin, this is what we see...

It's a total mess.

But here's the weird bit: nothing's been stolen.

CABIN FEVER BG EPS

Word spreads in a matter of seconds. Butch and Chuck are mortified and Tink's entourage are in a major flap. Blake's beside himself and Tink's mum is threatening to sue the captain.

It's all pretty dramatic stuff, but no one's been hurt. Nothing's even missing. Yet Tink's really upset. That's girls for you.

"Maybe I've got a stalker," she says. The heat is obviously causing her imagination to work overtime.

"There aren't any fans on board," I point out. "Just movie people. Target Films chartered the whole ship. There isn't anyone here but us."

Following us? I reckon Tink's being paranoid. "The boat's not there any more," I remind her.

"Well, maybe the man from it got on board during the night. Maybe he's hiding thomewhere wight now."

Yep. Definitely paranoid. And definitely imagining things. But I decide to humour her. "Could be, I suppose." Then I add, "He looked a bit like the guy I saw in the British Museum."

Tink reacts like this:

"You SAID he was obsethed with the necklace!" she gasps. "Of courthe, he wants to get his hands on this!" Tink's got the Anubis collar back on – she clapped it around her neck the second she saw it lying, untouched, on her bedside table in the middle of all that mess. But she's rubbing her neck crossly, as if it's choking her.

I say calmly, "You left it right there on the table while we were swimming. He can't possibly have missed it. So why didn't he take it?"

"I don't know," she says forlornly. "It's all vewy strange."

CAIRO

The cruise liner arrives in Cairo the next morning. It feels like we've been zapped from one century to another.

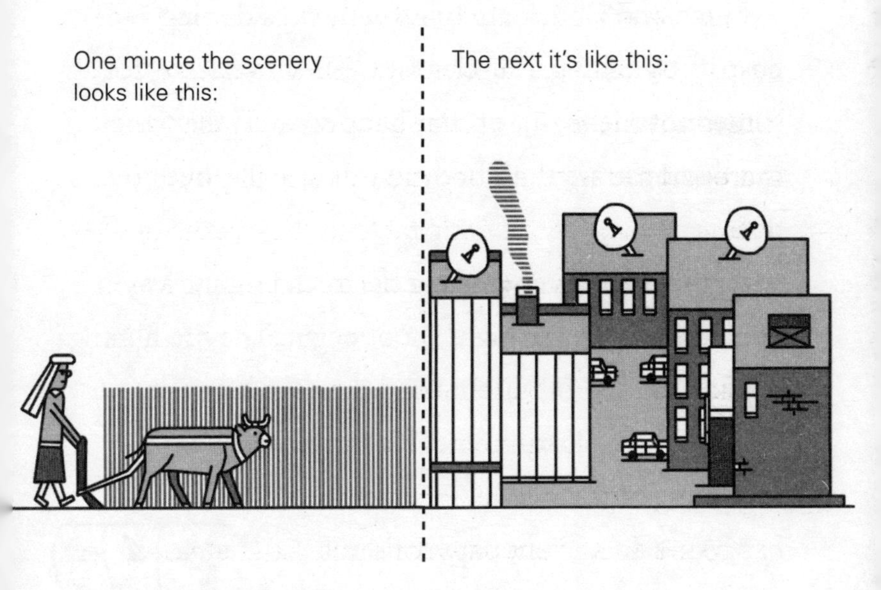

We're all transported to a five-star hotel in the city centre, megastars in limos, the rest of us on a coach.

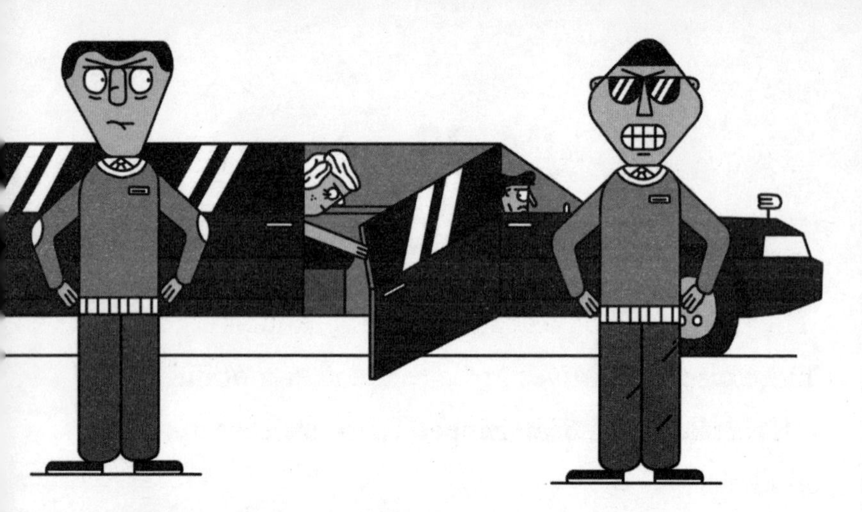

Butch and Chuck are fully alert, eyes darting, nostrils twitching, muscles taut. They're itching for someone to leap out of the shadows at Tink so they can demonstrate their bodyguarding skills, but no one does.

At the hotel, everyone checks in and right away preparations for the night shoot begin. They're filming outside the Cairo museum and there's a lot to do.

Tink's – aka Kitty's – next scene is from the beginning of the movie. Her father has found an ancient papyrus scroll and he and Kitty are taking it to the museum to show Professor Saleh, an Egyptology expert. Unfortunately the

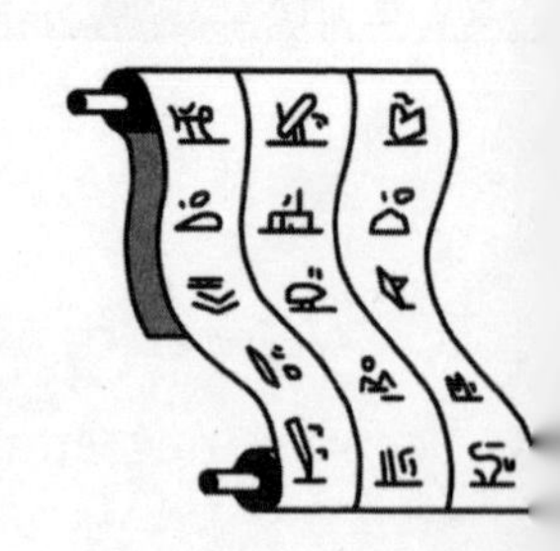

bad guys are already hot on their trail. Dan and Kitty meet Professor Saleh in the Tutankhamen section of the museum and he translates the hieroglyphs. The papyrus scroll reveals where the Anubis collar is hidden.

Professor Saleh is horrified.

Tomb of Doom!!! Scene 7 p. 45

PROF SALEH: You should not have unearthed this!

DAN DIAMOND: I'm an archaeologist. I dig things up, Professor. It's what I do.

PROF SALEH: Promise me one thing - you and your daughter must not go looking for this collar.

[Dan Diamond looks shifty.]

PROF SALEH: Did you not hear what the papyrus said? "The god demands one soul in exchange for another." The laws of the underworld cannot be flouted! This is no ordinary relic, Mr Diamond. You cannot conceive of the horror that will be unleashed if you proceed. You must destroy the scroll. Forget its existence. You are meddling with powers you do not understand...

As if to prove the point, the professor is then murdered right in front of them. It's well cool – an asp is poked through a ventilation grille in the wall and slithers up his trouser leg. After that, all hell breaks loose. There are machine-guns and explosions – the full works. Cue major destruction sequence as Dan and Kitty escape.

This is another word for an Egyptian cobra. When she was queen, Cleopatra tested poisons on criminals who'd been condemned to death. She decided that an asp bite was the best because it made victims sleepy and they died quite peacefully.

The Egyptian authorities weren't that wild about having a film crew bumbling around their ancient treasures, so the actual scene with Professor Saleh will be filmed in London. All Blake's doing tonight is shooting Dan and Kitty running hell for leather away from the museum building. The explosions will be added later with CGI.

Meanwhile, we've got the day free to do some more sightseeing. I'm all in favour of going to the pyramids. I read that you can go right down inside them and I reckon there are probably trapdoors and secret tunnels just waiting to be discovered, but Tink's not especially keen. "There might be thpiders!"

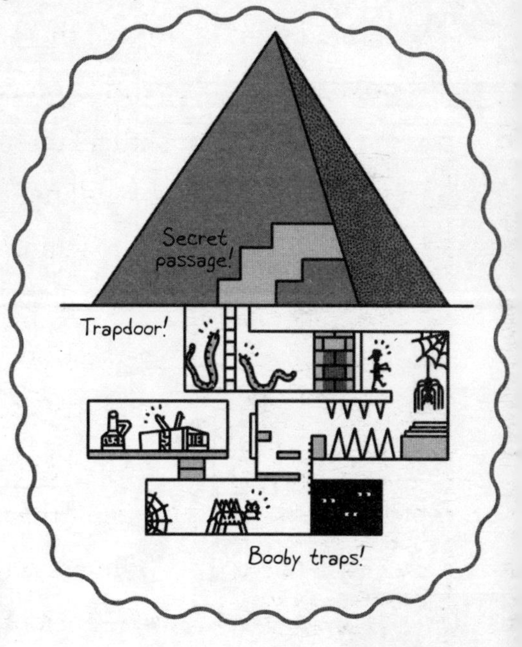

I chose the Valley of the Kings so I suppose it's her turn now. I steel myself for a day of shopping for pink sparkly things, but Tink surprises me.

"Let's go to the museum," she says. "I'd weally like to see the tweasures of Tutankhamen."

TREASURE PLANET

Sparks	**Dolly**	**Grip City**	**Craft services**	**The talent**
Electricians.	Camera platform on wheels.	Where the sparks stash their stuff.	Catering!	The actors.

The crew are setting up outside the museum. Tink and me and her mum and all her entourage pick our way between them and go on in.

I'm expecting the place to be crowded with tourists, but they seem more interested in standing around outside watching the film crew setting up.

We're in there for all of ten minutes before Museum Fatigue afflicts the grown-ups. Tink's mum starts yawning first and that sets off Donna and Trudi. Meanwhile, Butch and Chuck are walking slower and slower, and by the time me and Tink reach the Tutankhamen section they've all collapsed onto various benches.

This exhibition is pretty amazing. There are masses of statues and carvings of people and animals, plus loads of furniture.

We stop by a carving of a dog: 3,000 years old but it looks like it's about to spring off its box and sink its teeth into anyone who annoys it.

Anubis. That name again. It reminds me of the dog I kept seeing out of the corner of my eye back in Luxor. It sends a little prickle down my spine.

"It's sad to buwy these lovely things undergwound," says Tink.

I know what she means. It's kind of creepy – making all this stuff and then cramming it into a tomb to keep a dead guy company.

When we reach the jewellery cases, everything looks weirdly familiar, and I'm even more creeped out until Tink reminds me that the actors were wearing copies of this stuff when Blake filmed the sunrise scene last week.

At last we come to *that* mask. Pointing at the cobra on Tutankhamen's forehead, I tell Tink, "That was supposed to spit fire at his enemies."

Tink is unimpressed. "It didn't work, did it? Not if he was murdered."

I'm about to mention the curse and Carter's canary, but then we hear angry voices.

Instinctively we both duck down behind the mask. But through the case I can still see what's going on.

If this was a movie, at this point there would be sinister music setting your teeth on edge. My heart flips over and my eyes pop out. Because it really is him: the man I saw in London! Tink was right! He must have been following

MUSICAL MAESTRO

John Williams has written the soundtrack for gazillions of films, from *Harry Potter* to *Jaws*. He's had 48 Oscar nominations.

our boat. He's got one of the museum guards by his jumper and he's yelling at him in Arabic. I don't understand any of it.

But then, suddenly, I do. Just one word. From the safety demo on the plane. The Sinister Stranger is spitting it into the face of the guard.

The men forget their argument for a moment and turn to see Tink's mum fast approaching, Butch and Chuck at her heels. We can't pretend we're not here. We stand up and stroll casually towards Mrs Cherry.

Tink is a professional actress.

She confidently marches straight past the men, not giving either of them a glance.

As for me, I can't help looking up at the Sinister Stranger when I draw level with him.

His eyes narrow. He gives a slight nod. He's recognized me, too. Which for some reason makes me feel very nervous.

NIGHT AT THE MUSEUM 

Film sets are soooooo boring. While Tink's being made up, I'm standing around outside Dad's trailer kicking the dust into clouds. But I'd much rather be here than getting an early night back at the hotel. Until I've worked out why the Sinister Stranger is following us, I'm sticking with the crowd. I wish my pack brother was here to defend me.

The shot Blake's working on is a close-up of Dan and Kitty Diamond crashing through a window, then panning out to take in the whole building blowing up.

Once the CGI is added, it will look like this:

Ralph and Tink don't have any lines to say; they don't even actually have to jump through the window. All they have to do is lie down on the path as if they've just landed there, get up and then run like crazy without falling over.

Dad's finished Tink's make-up. Through the open door of his trailer I can see she's about to jump down from the swirly-whirly chair, when he says anxiously, "What's that?"

"What's what?"

"That. There."

"What, where?"

Dad's pointing at Tink's neck and suddenly everyone else in the trailer is trying to get a closer look.

For a moment I can't see what he's talking about. Then I notice a patch of red skin where her neck joins her shoulders.

"Heat rash?" says Mrs Cherry, looking concerned.

"Maybe." Dad knows a thing or two about skin. "Or some kind of allergic reaction. Better keep an eye on it."

Tink swears she's feeling fine, so everything proceeds as it should. It's dark now but as hot as ever. The ground is pumping out heat like a radiator on full-blast. Every two seconds, Dad has to dust Ralph Pitter's face with powder to soak up his sweat.

Everyone gets in position and the cameras roll, and the first take is going smoothly until they reach the sphinx. Then Ralph trips and falls flat on his face.

They have to do the take again. This means:

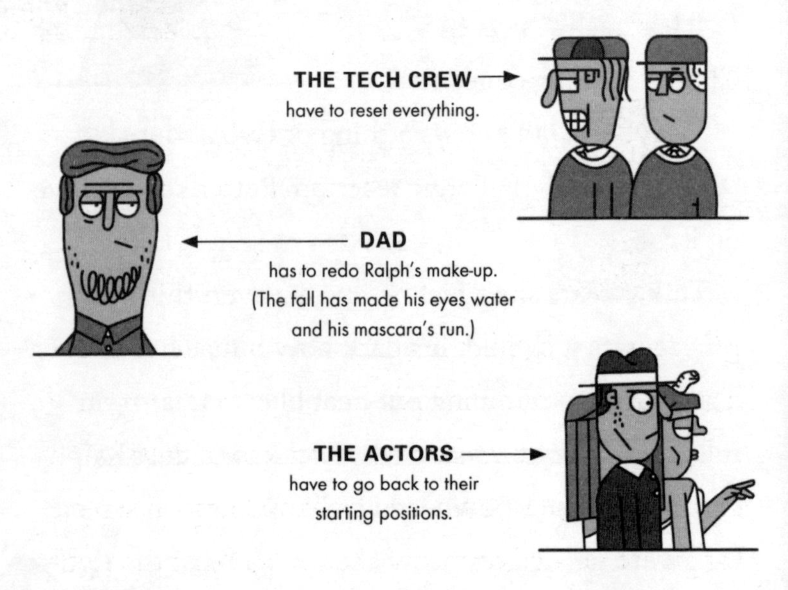

Then Mike, the cameraman, announces there's a problem with the dolly – it's not running smoothly, he says; grit has got into the machinery. Everyone looks at me. That is *so* unfair! No one told me that kicking up dust clouds was a crime.

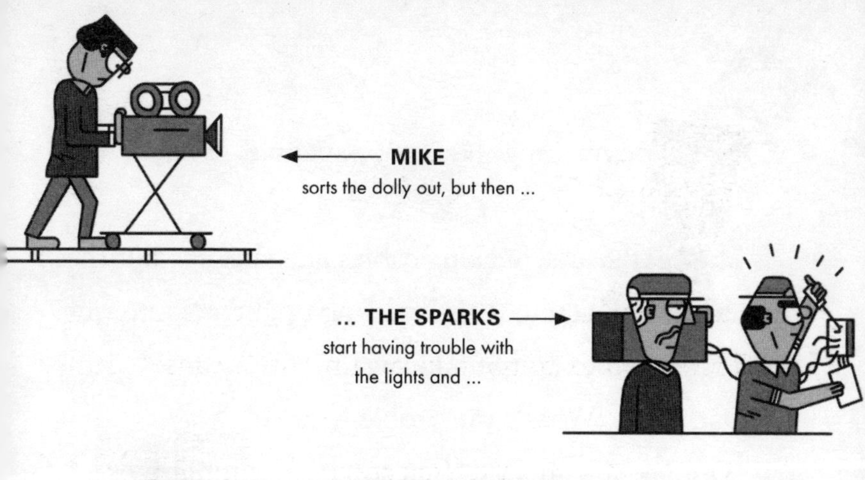

Everyone looks at me again. Surely I can't be held responsible for the electricity supply!

They can't film the scene without any lighting, because no one will see what's happening on screen. Lights are needed to throw shadows in just the right places, but they keep flickering and making this strange buzzing noise.

Dad's on stand-by. Me and Tink are sipping ice-cold drinks. Everyone is getting hot and bothered.

Blake's chewing his fingernails irritably and

demanding, "Come on, people! What's the hold-up?"

The sparks are checking cables and sockets, but the lights are still acting weird: getting brighter, sputtering and fading, then brightening again.

Dad says, "What's the problem, Sid?"

"Dunno," he growls. "I reckon it's the mummy's curse."

My ears prick up. I still haven't told Tink the story.

"Hey, Tink," I say. "Do you want to hear about Tutankhamen's curse?"

"Sam..." Dad says warningly.

But Tink cuts across him. Pulling herself up to her full height, she says imperiously, "What curthe? Tell me about it, Tham."

The Mighty Tink has spoken. Dad rolls his eyes but keeps quiet. Her wish is my command.

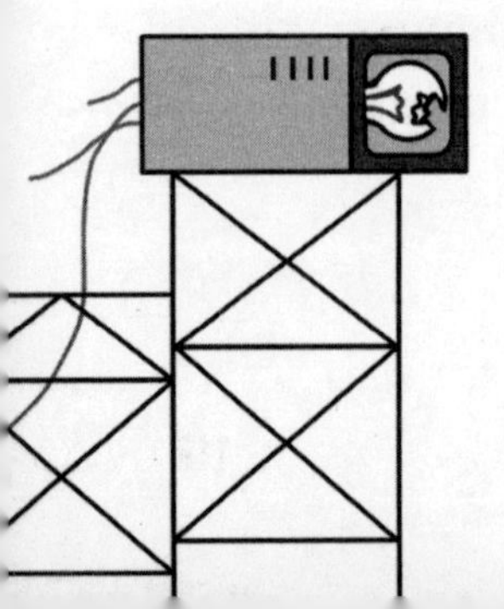

In hushed tones, I begin the story…

"The entrance to Tutankhamen's tomb was buried for years, then this guy Howard Carter decided to go looking for it.

This other guy, Lord Carnarvon, paid for the expedition. He was like the Money Man behind a movie.

So when he found the entrance, Carter phoned Carnarvon.

Both of them went into the tunnel. But they found this warning written on the wall – a curse."

THEY WHO ENTER
THIS SACRED TOMB
SHALL SWIFT BE
VISITED BY THE
WINGS OF DEATH.

"We didn't thee that," says Tink, eyes narrow with suspicion.

"Don't interrupt," I tell her.

"Poor cweature!"

Tink's right. Cursing people is one thing, but cursing a defenceless dog? That's just mean.

"And at that exact same moment," I continue, "every single light in Cairo went out."

As soon as the words leave my mouth there's a blinding flash, the lights on set go

… and we're all plunged into total darkness.

COBRA (BG) (F)

I yelp. Tink squeals and grabs my hand. Which makes me yelp again. There's a stunned silence, followed by whoops of laughter and howls of derision from the sound crew.

"You OK, Sam?" comes Dad's voice. "Just stand still. They'll get the power back on soon."

When my eyes adjust, I see it isn't completely dark: the moon's casting a silvery glow across the square. Sid's fiddling around with a cable and a screwdriver.

CURSES!

It was Conan Doyle – the guy who wrote the Sherlock Holmes books – who went around telling everyone there was a pharaoh's curse.

"Go on with the story," orders Tink.

"OK. Two weeks after they opened the tomb, Lord Carnarvon was bitten..."

"By a dog?"

"No, by a mosquito."

Tink seems disappointed, so I add, "The bite got infected and he dropped dead. Then five months later his brother died too."

Dad's staring at me. I can see exactly what he's thinking.

So I say, "It was just coincidence. I mean, Howard Carter lived to be really old—" I stop because I've suddenly remembered the canary. Dad stares at me. I shift uncomfortably from one foot to the other.

In the moonlight, Tink raises an eyebrow and waits.

I swallow nervously.

Tink puts her hands on her hips and gives me a look.

Reluctantly, I add, "OK... Howard Carter's canary died the day the tomb was opened. It got swallowed by a cobra."

"A COBWA?" Tink's eyes widen. We've both seen the mask of Tutankhamen with the cobra coiled on the brow – the one that was supposed to spit fire at his enemies. Who'd have thought it would single out a teeny-tiny canary?

Suddenly, as quickly as it went out, power is restored. The lights on set are back and so is every light in the museum. Plus its alarm is clanging at full volume. The noise is deafening.

Then I notice someone charging across the square. I swear it's the Sinister Stranger – and he seems to be running for his life. Anubis is chasing him! What on earth…?

Before I can work out what it means – before I can even point him out to Tink – there are suddenly loads of sirens, and police cars come screeching towards us, flashing lights, burning rubber.

I pick up that word again.

طوارئ! طوارئ!

Emergency!!! Emergency!!!

It seems the museum has been broken into. The whole film crew has to clear out of the square NOW!!

And the police aren't saying when – or if – we'll be allowed back.

DESERT THUNDER BG F

"Fancy a look at the pyramids?" asks Dad the next morning. The police are investigating the museum break-in, so he's got an unexpected day off.

My head is full of Anubis and Tutankhamen and the Sinister Stranger, but I'm still pretty keen to see the pyramids up close and it will be nice to hang out with Dad for a bit. Mrs Cherry has her heart set on a day's heavy-duty pampering in the hotel spa, so Tink decides to tag along with us. Naturally Chuck and Butch have to come too, and before long we're all being driven through the streets of Cairo in her limo. Dad's never ridden in a megastar's car, and he's impressed … until he discovers what's in the drinks cabinet.

We're all suddenly in a holiday mood and decide we need to see the pyramids in proper tourist style. The limo stops in a little square full of horses and camels and a lot of men shouting and yelling, desperately trying to outdo each other to get our attention.

Dad does the haggling. It's like watching some really bad acting.

Dad: How much for a camel ride?

Man:	For this very special, very noble animal, sir, it is 200 Egyptian pounds.
Dad:	You have got to be kidding!
Man:	It's a very nice camel, Mr Englishman. You see her teeth? Very strong, very good, very fine animal. The best in the whole of Egypt.
Dad:	I'll give you 20.
Man:	You want us to starve? I have a wife! Seven children! But for you, sir, I give a special price. 175.
Dad:	That's daylight robbery! 30.
Man:	I have a sick mother also. 150.
Dad:	You think I'm made of money? 40.
Man:	My father is on his deathbed. 150.

Twenty minutes later, Dad agrees a price and we each pick an animal.

Chuck and Butch opt for horses, but they're big and the horses aren't. The rest of us go for camels: me and Tink on one and Dad on another. It's easy enough to scramble into the saddle when their camels are lying down, but then the handlers order them to stand up. When our one gets to its feet, me and Tink lurch backwards and forwards so violently it's like being on a rollercoaster. Wa-haay!

I've never been on a camel before and love the idea of riding round the pyramids, but I seem to be the only one with a smile on my face.

This is how everyone else looks:

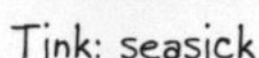

Tink: seasick

Dad: stressed

Chuck and Butch: embarrassed

With a guide leading the camels, we ride out of the square and soon buildings give way to sand. When we crest the hill – *bang!* – there are the pyramids. Behind them, stretching away as far as the eye can see, is nothing but desert.

The pyramids are brilliant, but the Sphinx is smaller than I was expecting. The guide takes us up to it and Dad gets off his camel to take a few pictures to send to Gran.

The events of last night are still going round in my head and I can't keep quiet any longer. I turn and whisper to Tink, "It must have been the Sinister Stranger breaking into the museum!"

SHORT AND SWEET

The Sphinx isn't the only thing that's smaller than you expect when you see it up close. Loads of famous screen giants are practically pocket-sized. Johnny Depp is 5′8″. Tom Cruise is 5′7″. Daniel Radcliffe is only 5′5″.

"Don't be thilly, Tham," Tink snaps. She's really grumpy today. "He wouldn't have argued with the guard if he was planning a wobbery."

"I saw him running away, though! He was being chased by a dog."

"A dog? What sort?"

"Don't know. It looked like Anubis. You know – that carving of the tomb guardian."

Tink pales. "Like the cobwa that killed the canary!" she gasps faintly. "The dog was protecting the tweasure! It's Tutankhamen's curthe!"

Maybe she's right. Because just then Tink's eyes roll right back into her head and she slides sideways off the camel, landing in the sand with a soft *plop!*

EMERGENCY CALL

Butch and Chuck are now ready to kill:

Luckily, before the pair of them can begin, Tink stirs in the sand. Her eyelids flutter and she says, "Tham? Marcuth? Oh dear! I feel vewy funny." Her voice is weak and wobbly and suddenly she bursts into tears. "I want my mummy!"

Then she faints again.

Tink's collapse creates a full-scale emergency. It's like being back in the museum square. Sirens, flashing lights, the works. The next thing I know, me and Dad are in the As-Salam International Hospital canteen, waiting to hear the news from Tink's bedside. People keep sidling up to us.

You know Tinkerbelle Cherry? What's she like? I mean, really?

It's both scary and odd – she's unconscious and no one knows why. For what seems like hours the whole

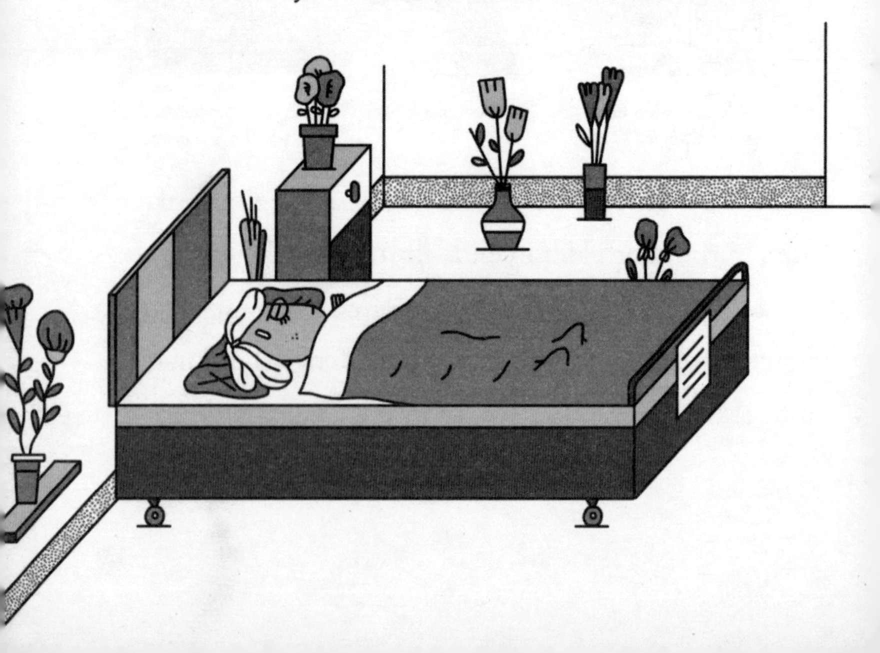

building echoes with the sound of her mum's hysterics. Then eventually Tink comes round and we're allowed to go and see her.

After a lot of poking and prodding, the doctors have decided that it's nothing too awful – she's not going to die or anything, which is a big relief. But she's a bit feverish and her neck's covered in little blisters. The reason for her sudden illness turns out to be this: She's had a severe allergic reaction to the Anubis collar.

RASH MOVES

The actor who originally played the part of the Tin Man in *THE WIZARD OF OZ* had to drop out of the movie after being hospitalized for an allergy to the aluminium dust in his make-up.

THE HOAX

BG 5Z

Tink is nothing if not professional. Her only thought is, The show musthe go on. She doesn't want to disrupt the shooting schedule, so she only spends one night in hospital. In the morning, she's looking pale and there are dark shadows under her eyes, but she's ready to go the moment Target Films is allowed back to the museum. Meanwhile, I am required to Amuse Her.

We hang out in her hotel room and I behave in a manner worthy of a saint. Barbie and Ken have a nice relaxing time on vacation with Edward and Bella in the south of France. All morning!!! They have about a billion costume changes, but I am patient and kind and do every single one without complaining. The halo above my head is lit by a million volts of virtue. I am so angelic I can feel my wings starting to grow.

However, I draw the line at eating lunch Tink-style. When her chef appears with a bowl of softly steaming lentils, I say Dad's expecting me and leave so fast there are clouds of dust all along the corridor behind me.

But the Target Films crew aren't having the long, leisurely lunch I expected. They're grabbing bread rolls from the restaurant buffet, stuffing them in their pockets and heading out of the door. Because it turns out that the police have lifted their ban: filming can carry on this evening. The whole thing was a hoax, Dad informs me. Someone deliberately

SPEED STEALING

In 2012, it took thieves only 120 seconds to snatch artefacts worth two million pounds from the Oriental Museum in Durham.

shorted the power supply then smashed one of the museum's windows. Nothing was stolen.

"That's a bit weird, isn't it?" I say.

Dad shrugs. He's not very interested. He has his mind on higher things, like prosthetic noses and sweat-absorbent face powder. But I'm wondering if the Sinister Stranger's behind it and what he might do next. And without Watson, my trusty sidekick, there's no one for this particular Sherlock to talk to.

LAST GASP

Filming kicks off again that same evening. I ride with Tink in her limo from the hotel to the museum and I'm surprised to see she's wearing the Anubis collar. Craig has had the genius idea of sticking a leather "shield" to the back of it so it won't come into contact with her skin. She doesn't seem very thrilled, though. She's plucking at it irritably the whole way and when we pull up outside the museum, she says, "It's not wight, Tham."

"What's not white?"

Tink looks furious. She stamps her foot and tugs at the necklace. "Not WHITE! It's not RIGHT!"

"Oh. Sorry. Do you mean the necklace?" A dim memory stirs somewhere at the back of my mind: didn't the Sinister Stranger use those very words just before he went beserk in the British Museum? I'm about to tell Tink, but she's already out of the limo and heading towards Dad's trailer to be made up.

When Ralph and Tink are in place, filming begins.

The cameras are rolling. I'm standing watching when I feel something pressing itself into the palm of my hand. Something cold. And wet. And alive.

It's not like I *meant* to ruin a perfect take. But when something cold and wet unexpectedly forces itself into your hand in the dark at night and then *breathes* on you, how can anyone help screaming?

"Cut!" shouts Blake. "For God's sake, cut! And get that blasted kid out of here."

I just register that the thing in my hand is a nose, and that the nose belongs to the Anubis dog – who isn't looking cursed or revengeful or even faintly supernatural and, in fact, seems to be as friendly as Watson – when Dad puts me in a taxi and dispatches me back to the hotel. I barely have time to draw breath.

Out of the taxi window I see the Sinister Stranger standing in the shadows, the dog now at his side, tail wagging.

But the man's not looking at the dog or watching the filming like the rest of the crowd. He's staring at Anoushka's wardrobe trailer.

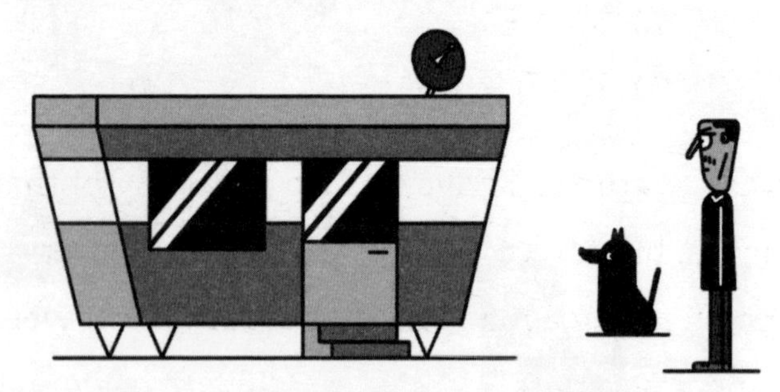

HOMEWARD BOUND

WLI

When I get back to the hotel, I start making notes. It's what Sherlock Holmes would do. This is what I know so far:

1) The Sinister Stranger (hereafter referred to as SS) was at the British Museum.

2) SS followed us up the Nile.

3) SS disappeared before Tink's cabin was raided.

4) SS is now here in Cairo.

5) SS is obsessed with the necklace.

6) So is Tink.

7) SS has a dog.

Point 7 is crucial. I have no idea what any of that list means, but I have a detective's instinct about number 7: surely a man who has a dog with a wet nose and a waggy tail cannot be All Bad?

TECHNICAL HITCH

When they were filming *JAWS*, the crew had so many problems with the mechanical shark that the shoot went up from the 55 days they'd planned to 159 days. The original budget doubled.

The rest of the night's filming goes smoothly according to Dad. I'm asleep when he finally gets back to the hotel, but the next morning he tells me that Blake is so happy with what he's shot, we can go back to England. They're ahead of schedule, which is something of a miracle. Films hardly ever come in on time and on budget so this is probably a first in the whole of movie history. It's certainly never happened to Dad before.

While the production assistants are running around like mad things arranging flights, the rest of the crew spend the day chilling by the hotel pool.

The thought of being reunited with Watson has pushed the strange events of the past few days to the back of my mind. Dad's having a race with Craig and Sid, and I'm lying on a sun-lounger with my eyes shut.

Then a shadow falls across me. I open my eyes. Tink is standing there, lower lip thrust out, *glowering* as only Tinkerbelle Cherry can.

```
Sam:   You OK, Tink?
Tink:  No, I'm not. I don't like
       this.
Sam:   Well, take it off then.
```

Typical! She loved that necklace a week ago, and now she's gone off it. That's actresses for you: fickle.

Tink unclasps the necklace, holds it in both hands and says yet again, "It's not right."

I sit up.

Sam: Funny, that. It's what the Sinister Stranger said before he went crazy and attacked the guard at the British Museum.

Tink: [Eyes narrowed.] And he was there when the Cairo museum was bwoken into?

Sam: But nothing was stolen. It's weird. Nothing was taken from your cabin and nothing was stolen from the British Museum either.

Tink: You mean that was bwoken into too?!

Sam: Yeah. The week before I was there.

Tink's now put the collar back on and is looking excited. "I suthpect—"

Just then her mum comes over to say that everything's sorted out for Tink's flight to London, then she settles herself down on a nearby sun-lounger.

Tink's forehead is furrowed as if she's thinking. Suddenly she beams at her mother…

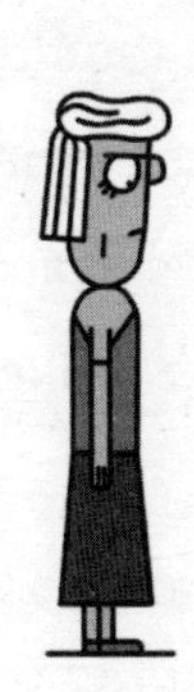

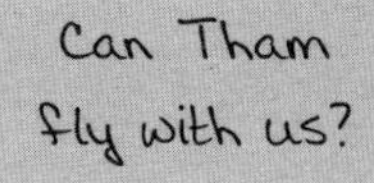

Mrs Cherry looks a bit surprised. Tink usually travels megastar-style in her own private jet with just her entourage for company.

"There won't be room for him, honey."

"But he's my vewy best fwiend! Donna and Twudi can go on a different airplane, can't they? Just this once?"

Tink's PA and stylist look a bit put out, but they can't say anything.

Tink hasn't finished yet. "And there'll be woom for one more, won't there?" she says, giving an Oscar-winning performance of a sweet, thoughtful child. "Why don't we ask Anoushka to come too? She's been vewy sick."

"Tinky, you're an angel! That would be kind."

Anoushka looks slightly baffled when Mrs Cherry invites her onto their plane, but she accepts without hesitation. The Mighty Tink has spoken. Anoushka hasn't really got any choice.

Tink gives me a Very Significant Look.

Which is all very well. But I haven't a clue what she's on about.

The interior of Tink's private plane is as girlie and sparkly and over the top as you'd expect. Even the pilot is in a satin, sequined uniform. Dad gives the guy a sideways look when he drops me off and mutters under his breath, "Whatever they're paying you, mate, it's nowhere near enough."

Dad and the rest of the cast and crew are on a flight that leaves half an hour after ours. Gran's coming to collect me and Dad, so I have strict instructions to find her in the arrivals hall and then wait for him.

On board, everything's supremely luxurious, but it's still pretty crowded. There's no way me and Tink can have a proper talk, so I go and explore instead. It turns out there's – get this! – a bathroom with a Jacuzzi in it and about sixty different kinds of soap! You don't need to bother with towels because there's a walk-in hairdryer thing which blasts you from head to toe.

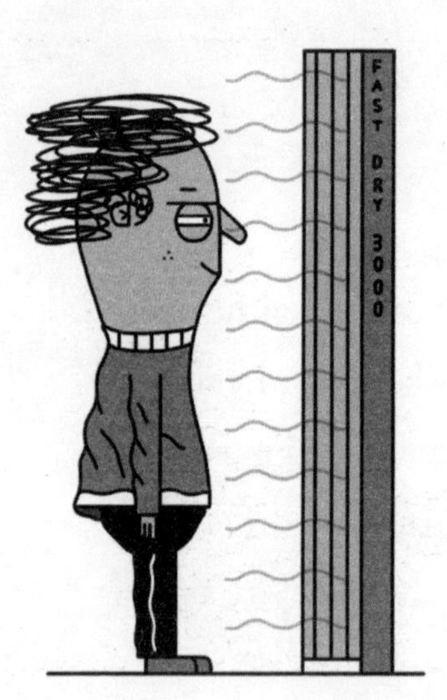

Chuck and Butch have made themselves comfortable on the sofa. Anoushka squeezes in between them and Mrs Cherry is sitting up at the front near the pilot, which means I can try out all the chairs. There are two in the middle that are big and

squashy and spin full-circle. You can get up quite a speed if you try hard enough.

Then there are the chairs at the front, where you can watch back-to-back Disney Princess films on a pop-up cinema screen. I press a button on the side and the seat does this:

The plane even has one of those massage chairs.

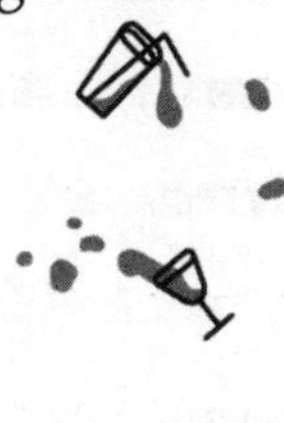

I'm having so much fun that I forget there's no escaping Tink's chef when you're in the air, 25,000 feet above the nearest burger bar.

When we land, I'm feeling slightly sick. But I'm so excited about seeing Watson that I don't care. I hope Gran has brought him along with her to the airport. It will be a fifty-Kleenex reunion, guaranteed. (Bigger than *Bolt*. Warmer than *Eight Below*. Waggier than *101 Dalmations*. Lickier than *Lassie Come Home*.)

Superstars don't need to bother with all the boring standing around waiting for bags to come down conveyor belts; I've got my case with me already. Once we've sped through passport control, I'm off at a run. I don't wait for Tink because I know Gran has brought my pack brother to meet me. I can feel Watson out there, waiting. I barely hear Tink hissing, "Tham! Come back! We have to watch Anoushka!"

UNDERDOG WLI

Dogs aren't really allowed at airports unless they're travelling, but Gran's not the kind of woman that airport officials argue with.

Watson must have caught my scent: he starts barking as soon as I've got through into arrivals. Gran can't hang on to thirty kilos of dog, so he comes hurtling through the crowd.

He is wearing a new expression. Number 13: *RAPTUROUS!!!*

When he sees me he does an *Underdog*-style take-off.

I dodge. If he connects, I'll end up with a nosebleed.

He smashes into the man behind me. Luckily he's pretty fat, so Watson's not hurt. My dog is in ecstasies. He's rolling around on his back and then jumping up and then rolling around again, and all the time he's barking and saying:

I thought you had gone for ever and I was so very very sad and lonely I have been howling all night every night!! Where have you been? Why oh why oh why did you leave me with She Who Shouts and Smells of Toast?

I'm down on the floor making a big fuss of him, but then Watson remembers:

Pants + Sam = Treat

He shoots off to see what he can find.

It's only then that I realize the person he knocked over is the American guy we saw in Tutankhamen's tomb. His wife is with him and neither of them are looking very friendly. What are they doing here?

"Tham!" Tink's followed me. She must have run on ahead of Chuck and Butch. Big Mistake. All around the arrivals hall, autograph-hunters are already pulling pens from their pockets and advancing towards her.

Watson is crashing through the crowd on a desperate quest for pants when he bashes into Anoushka. She shrieks, falls over and drops her suitcase. The contents spill across the lino. Watson snatches up a pair of knickers and brings them back to me. He drops them into my hands, grinning with insane delight.

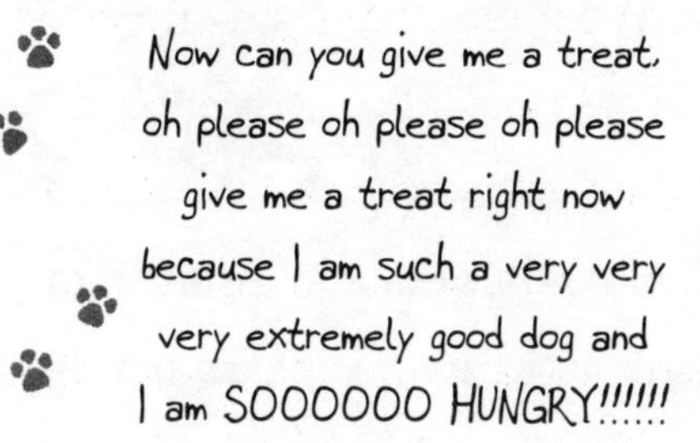

I go to hand the pants straight back but my finger catches on something sharp. Like a tooth. Then I see a glint of gold. There's something wrapped up in them. It's the Anubis collar! *What…?*

Because here's the weird bit: Tink's already got it on.

TWINS (F)

How can there be two Anubis collars? Anoushka told Craig there wasn't a spare – we heard her on the boat. Why would she lie about it?

The fat Americans are looming over me and Watson. What's up with them? The man snarls, **"That's mine, kid. Hand it over."**

"Tham, don't!" yells Tink. She can't move for fans.

"Give it to me. Now!"

"Don't listen to them!" screams Tink. "They're wobbers!"

"What's going on over there?" calls Gran. "Are you all right, Samuel?"

Tink's doing her best to get to me, but right now it's just me and the fat Americans. And Anoushka. She's managed to fight her way through the crowd and she's looking mean.

Watson is still waiting for his treat, but he's not stupid. He's noticed that Menace is in the air. Suddenly he looks a lot like Anubis. When Anoushka and the fat Americans all try to grab the necklace, he makes like a crocodile.

He's all teeth and slobber. He doesn't actually bite any of them, but they back off.

Tink's finally reached us. She yells, "Wun, Tham! Wun!!"

Anoushka and the fat Americans wouldn't dare to hurt either of us in front of witnesses, but that doesn't seem to occur to me or Tink. They glare at us, eyes glinting with fury, and we both panic – and scarper, ducking under the barrier, sprinting back though passport control and towards baggage reclaim.

Mistake #1

Running away from just about anybody who could actually help us.

Definitely NOT what Sherlock would do.

The Americans are surprisingly fast.

So is Anoushka.

They're hard on our heels and Watson has another new expression. Number 14: *Baffled.* (He's not the only one.)

He thinks we're playing chase, but he's not entirely convinced this is a game.

Are they playing? Are they? Are they?
Or are they attacking? Are they enemies?
Shall I bite them? Shall I? Shall I?

Then:

Can I have my treat yet? Can I? Can I?
I'm SOOO HUNGRY I'M ALMOST FAINTING!!

At baggage reclaim the exit's blocked by another wall of people: Dad's flight has landed. Ahead of us is a whole planeload of passengers who'd be happy to save me and Tink.

So what do we do?

Mistake #2

Running in the opposite direction.

Tink and I seem to have lost any ability to think straight.

The conveyor belt sparks into life, ready to spew out suitcases.

Tink grabs my hand, I grab Watson and the three of us leap onto the conveyor belt and are carried out of baggage reclaim.

FLIGHT OF FANCY

In *Toy Story* 2 an airport announcement is made for Lasset Air flight 113. That's a reference to the film's director, John Lasseter.

At this point I don't really get why they're after us. I know they want the necklace and I'd be quite happy to give it to them. It's only a bit of jewellery! If I had any spare breath, I'd tell Tink. But she's a girl and girls are funny about stuff like that. So instead, this happens…

The conveyor belt loops round and carries us right back to baggage reclaim ...
... where the fat Americans are waiting!
We run.
The Americans are catching up.
This way!
Suddenly we're on the runway.
But we still haven't shaken them off!

We keep running ...

... and end up on a plane!

The crew aren't exactly pleased to see us.

Not pleased at ALL.
Emergency lever

The escape chute inflates.

We're out of here!

But straight back into danger.

The Americans have guns.
And they've grabbed Watson!

The game is up.

But then...
It is now!

You guys are ancient history.

RPOW!

END OF THE GAME

We've brought the airport to a complete standstill. An army of cops have us surrounded. A senior-looking policeman demands an explanation – NOW!!!!

I open my mouth and then close it again. I have nothing to say.

Tink steps forward, takes the Anubis collar from me and says to the policeman, "I think this is vewy valuable."

Before she can hand it over, the Sinister Stranger snatches the necklace from Tink, pulls out his eyeglass and has a good look at it.

A broad grin spreads across his face. He does a little dance on the spot. He's so excited that Watson catches his mood and plants his front feet on the Sinister Stranger's chest to give his face a good lick. The man doesn't mind. In fact, he laughs, rubs Watson's ears and calls him a very good dog. (A man who does that cannot possibly be a Bad Guy. Can he?)

Then he says, "Yes, this is right. It is the real thing. 3,000 years old. Priceless. It was removed from the British Museum the week before my visit. There was a break-in, was there not?"

Well, I don't know how Tink's managed to work that out. And before anyone can say another word, the police decide to slap all the grown-ups in handcuffs and take them in for questioning. It's hours before me, Dad and Watson are allowed to go home and a whole week before I get to see Tink again.

When we do finally meet up it's at the film studio. Tink's had a busy morning being dangled upside down and threatened with sacrifice, but after lunch she's free, so we decide to take Watson for a walk in the grounds. Dad and Tink's mum come along too and between us we piece the whole fiendishly cunning plot together.

It turns out that in real life it involved:

A fearlessly cool professor of ancient Egyptian history called Omar Bomani (aka the Sinister Stranger), who noticed that the Anubis collar in the British Museum was a fake but couldn't get the guards to believe him. He decided to take matters into his own hands.

A creepy villain (aka Anoushka, part-time wardrobe mistress, full-time Criminal Mastermind), who had two copies of the Anubis collar made. The first got put in the British Museum when the original was stolen, the second was for Tink to wear during shooting.

Her partners in crime – the fat Americans. Anoushka had arranged to smuggle the real collar out to Egypt among the *TOMB OF DOOM!!!* costumes and props. She was going to hand it over to them in Luxor, only she went down with food poisoning and Tink ended up wearing it by mistake.

A cute child star (aka Tinkerbelle Cherry), who turned out to be allergic to cheap metal. When Anoushka recovered from her illness, she broke into Tink's cabin and switched the real necklace with the second replica, which is why Tink suddenly came out in blisters halfway through filming. The ancient collar was gold, the replica wasn't.

TOMB ROBBERS

Thieves have always wanted to get their hands on Tutankhamen's treasures. His tomb was first robbed before he was even buried!

And there's more. It seems it wasn't just the Anubis collar the Americans were after. The police told Butch (who told Chuck, who told Donna, who told Mrs Cherry, who told the rest of us) that the American couple had been after the whole of Tutankhamen's jewellery collection. Anoushka was responsible for the power failure in Cairo and the attempted break-in, but she didn't get to steal anything because the Sinister Stranger and his dog* turned up. After that, he was keeping such a close eye on her that she didn't dare try again.

Fiendishly cunning, or what? And Anoushka would probably have got away with the whole thing if my pack brother hadn't retrieved the Anubis collar from her bag.

So that's it. The Sinister Stranger turned out to be the good guy, the wardrobe mistress turned out to be the villain, Watson's thieving turned out to be useful

* His dog is called Rameses. Omar Bomani (SS) has loads of photos of him on his phone.

and Tink and I turned out to be heroes who thwarted an international crime ring.

Confusing, huh? But that's the way it is in the movies.

TOMB OF DOOM!!!

Dan Diamond,
the fearlessly cool hero
RALPH PITTER

Kitty Diamond,
the hero's cute-as-cherry-pie daughter
TINKERBELLE CHERRY

Heston Schweinhund,
the Hitler-worshipping baddie
BEN SILVERMAN

•••

Producer
CAROL KLEIN

Director
BLAKE FORD

Wardrobe Mistress
ANOUSHKA KAMUN

Wardrobe Assistant
CRAIG GETTY

Special Effects Make-up Manager
MARCUS SWANN

Hair Stylist
KAREN WINFORD

Cinematographer
HOWELL PODER

Sound Engineer
DAVE BENGAL

Chief Electrician
SID BISHOP

Cameraman
MIKE ORCHARD

No pyramids were harmed in the making of this film.

DON'T TRY THIS AT HOME!

HOW TO EMBALM A PHARAOH

1.

Check he is properly dead.

2.

Remove his internal organs (apart from the heart – that gets weighed by Anubis later)

... and stuff him full of spices.

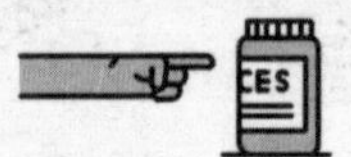

3.

Cover him with natron (that's like salt) and leave for several days until he's dried out.

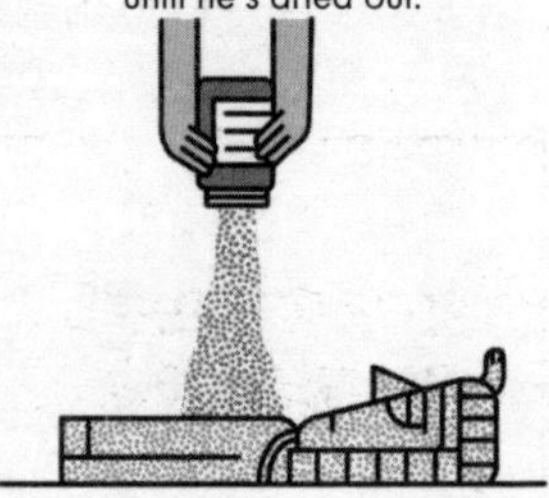

4.

Get a priest to open his mouth so he can eat and drink in the next life.

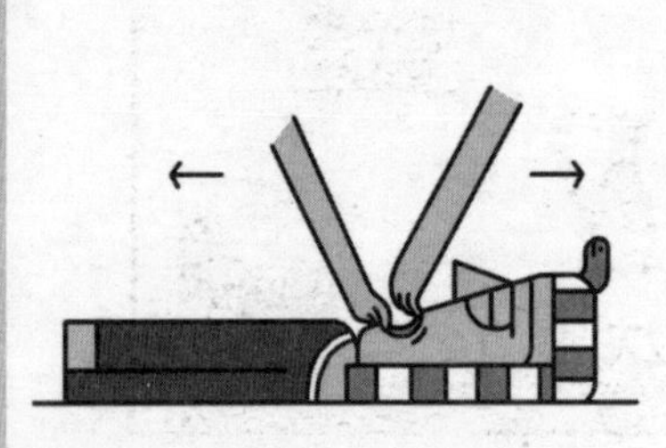

5.

Give him a wash, rub him with oil, wrap him in bandages and cover his face with a mask.

HOW TO EMBALM A PHARAOH

DON'T TRY THIS AT HOME!

6.
Put him in a coffin.

7.
Put that coffin inside another coffin.

8.
And another.

9.
Keep going as long as you want.

10.
Bury the coffin in a tomb with all the things he'll need for the next life. Including his servants.

FILM LIST

THE HISTORY BOYS 15

Comedy drama 2006 UK/US Colour 107 mins

Logline: Eight students have to pass an exam.

GODS AND MONSTERS 15

Drama 1998 US/UK Colour 105 mins

Logline: Biopic of James Whale – the film director who made *FRANKENSTEIN*.

BROTHER BEAR U

Animation 2003 US Colour 85 mins

Logline: Boy gets turned into bear and meets lots of talking animals.

THE MUMMY 15

Horror 1932 US B&W 73 mins

Logline: Egyptian mummy gets revived and thinks modern-day heroine is reincarnation of his ancient love.

DOG DAY AFTERNOON 15

Crime drama 1975 US Colour 119 mins

Logline: Guy plans robbery to pay for sex-change operation.

AIRBORNE PG

Drama 1993 US Colour 86 mins

Logline: Teenager moves house and has to swap his surfboard for rollerblades.

STAR WARS

Massive series of sci-fi epics

Logline: Goodies versus baddies in space.

VALLEY OF THE DOLLS 15

Drama 1967 US Colour 123 mins

Logline: Wannabe starlets claw their way to fame.

THE TEMPLE OF DOOM PG

Adventure 1984 US Colour 118 mins

Logline: Indiana Jones is at it again!

DAWN OF THE DEAD 18

Horror 2004 US Colour 100 mins

Logline: People run away from plague of zombies.

THE JEWEL OF THE NILE PG

Adventure 1985 US Colour 106 mins

Logline: Sequel to *ROMANCING THE STONE*.

VALLEY OF THE KINGS U

Romantic adventure 1954 US Colour 85 mins

Logline: Handsome archaeologist falls foul of tomb robbers.

STAR KID PG

Sci-fi 1997 US Colour 101 mins

Logline: Bullied kid finds alien combat suit and puts it on.

MIRAGE (UNCLASSIFIED)

Thriller 1965 US Colour 108 mins

Logline: Amnesiac man in paranoid nightmare.

THE SHIPPING NEWS 15

Drama 2001 US Colour 111 mins

Logline: Widowed man returns home to fishing village to start new life.

FILM LIST

TO CATCH A THIEF PG
Thriller 1955 US Colour 102 mins
Logline: Retired jewel thief has to catch copycat criminal.

CABIN FEVER 15
Horror 2002 US Colour 93 mins
Logline: Five friends are struck down by flesh-eating virus.

CAIRO (UNCLASSIFIED)
Crime drama 1963 US/UK B&W 90 mins
Logline: Master criminal decides to steal Tutankhamen's treasures.

TREASURE PLANET U
Animation 2002 US Colour 91 mins
Logline: Sci-fi version of *TREASURE ISLAND*.

NIGHT AT THE MUSEUM PG
Adventure 2006 US Colour 104 mins
Logline: Nightwatchman discovers museum exhibits come to life.

COBRA 18
Thriller 1986 US Colour 83 mins
Logline: Cop investigates murder and mayhem.

DESERT THUNDER 15
Thriller 1999 US Colour 90 mins
Logline: Retired pilot plots assault on secret chemical weapons plant.

EMERGENCY CALL U
Drama 1952 UK B&W 90 mins
Logline: Child with rare condition needs to find blood donor.

THE HOAX 15
Drama 2006 US Colour 116 mins
Logline: Failing author persuades publisher he's working on book about famous millionaire recluse and gets paid a fortune.

LAST GASP 18
Horror 1995 US Colour 93 mins
Logline: Bad guy kills tribe for their land and becomes possessed by one of their spirits.

HOMEWARD BOUND U
Adventure 1993 US Colour 84 mins
Logline: Bunch of cute animals go on incredible journey.

AIRPORT PG
Disaster movie 1970 US Colour 137 mins
Logline: Blizzards, bombs and bad guys cause airport chaos.

UNDERDOG U
Adventure 2007 US Colour 84 mins
Logline: Puppy gets superpowers after laboratory explosion.

TWINS PG
Comedy 1988 US Colour 102 mins
Logline: Non-identical twins team up to find their long-lost mother.

END OF THE GAME (UNCLASSIFIED)
Drama 1975 German Colour 106 mins
Logline: Dying policeman makes one last attempt to catch master criminal.

Tanya has written many books for children, including the award-winning Poppy Fields murder mystery series, *Waking Merlin*, *Merlin's Apprentice*, *The Kraken Snores*, *The World's Bellybutton* and three stories for younger readers featuring the characters Flotsam and Jetsam.

She is excited about writing Sam Swann's Movie Mysteries. "I love the movies (it's hard not to when you have an actor uncle who gets eaten by a mechanical shark!*) but I've always been as interested in the backstage stuff as what's on screen. I've got two children – both boys – and two Labradors. Sam and Watson are totally based on them and what they might get up to if they were ever let loose on a film set." Tanya is currently writing the third book in the series – which involves a stupendous superhero, some spectacular flying sequences and a murderous Ninja kitten.

Tanya also writes for young adults. You can find out more about all of her books at:

www.tanyalandman.com

---

* Robert Shaw, who played Quint in *JAWS*.